'You weren'
happened si:

Malcom was stil.

'Nor were you,' she replied. 'That doesn't change the fact that it was wrong.'

'Wrong then.'

'Yes.'

'But there's nothing wrong with what we're doing now, is there? Fostering a successful friendship…between our two daughters. Don't get tense about it, please. Don't act as if there's something dangerous about it.'

After living in the USA for nearly eight years, **Lilian Darcy** is back in her native Australia with her American historian husband and their four young children. More than ever, writing is a treat for her now, looked forward to and luxuriated in like a hot bath after a hard day. She likes to create modern heroes and heroines with good doses of zest and humour in their make-up, and relishes the opportunity that the Medical™ series gives her for dealing with genuine, gripping drama in romance and in daily life. She finds research fascinating too—everything from attacking learned medical tomes to spending a day in a maternity ward.

Recent titles by the same author:

WINNING HER BACK
THE MARRIAGE OF DR MARR
THE COURAGE TO SAY YES
HER PASSION FOR DR JONES

THE TRUTH
ABOUT CHARLOTTE

BY
LILIAN DARCY

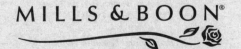

MILLS & BOON®

First published in Great Britain 2000
Harlequin Mills & Boon Limited,
Eton House, 18-24 Paradise Road, Richmond, Surrey TW9 1SR

© Lilian Darcy 2000

ISBN 0 263 82273 7

Set in Times Roman 10½ on 12 pt.
03-0011-48391

Printed and bound in Spain
by Litografia Rosés, S.A., Barcelona

CHAPTER ONE

'YOU'RE going to ring Ellie's house *right now*, aren't you, Mummy?' The pleading, persistent little voice came from right in front of the cupboard which Lucy needed to open in order to extract a saucepan.

'Yes, love,' she answered absently, then, too late, realised what she'd said. She tried to backtrack. 'That is, not exactly *right* now, but in a—'

'But you *said*. And you'd already said half an hour ago that you'd do it in ten minutes, which means you're twenty minutes late.'

Not for the first time, Lucy reflected that having an extremely intelligent child could be a mixed blessing. Charlotte was only five. It might have been easier on a single parent if she weren't so adept at doing things like subtracting ten minutes from half an hour to leave twenty minutes, and keeping track of every hasty parental promise ever made to her.

'All right, then, darling-heart...' It seemed easier to capitulate and make the promised phone call.

After all—with a twinge of remorse—she *had* 'said', and she did try to teach her daughter that one's word was one's bond.

'Here's the number. But I think I got the five back to front. Ellie says I did.' Charlotte thrust a grubby scrap of paper into Lucy's hand and led her, with a very crumpling grip on her skirt, to the phone.

Suppressing a sigh, Lucy picked it up and dialled, while Charlotte stood an inch away, gazing upwards with huge, hopeful blue eyes. The instrument rang eight times at the other end, and Lucy was just about to conclude with guilty relief that Ellie and her parents weren't at home when there was a click and the sound of a male voice.

Definitely a male voice, although what exactly it had said beyond 'Hello' Lucy didn't know, as the potatoes had just boiled over on the stove and the front doorbell had pealed, masking the words.

Flustered, and forgetting her phone etiquette entirely, she demanded distractedly, 'Um, is that Ellie's dad?'

'Yes, it is.'

'Well, uh, this is Charlotte's mother from school… No, don't answer the door, love. I'm not sure who it could be. But could you switch off the front burner on the stove? And as you might know by this time, she'd love to have Ellie over to play, and I thought—'

The doorbell pealed again, and the sudden hiss and splutter of steaming potato water onto the gas flame made Charlotte squeal and back away, giving Lucy further cause for remorse about her daughter. She really shouldn't have asked a five-year-old to tackle the stove, not with her own experience in rural emergency nursing. She knew only too well how easily a child could get burnt.

'Don't worry about it, Charlotte,' she instructed quickly.

Abandoning the potatoes to their fate, she focused on the phone conversation, and somehow she and Ellie's dad stumbled through an arrangement. Perhaps fortunately, it sounded as if there was almost as much chaos at the other end of the phone as there was at hers, but through it all they managed to agree that Ellie would come home after school with Charlotte tomorrow.

'Lovely!' Lucy said, and Charlotte correctly interpreted this as reason to start jumping up and down, excitedly clapping her hands.

'Oh, goody, goody, *goody*!'

Over the noise, Lucy heard, 'As you know, Ellie usually has a babysitter before and after school. Jenny has mentioned you very favourably, by the way.'

'Yes, we've chatted several times at bell-time over the past two weeks,' Lucy agreed.

But it was possible that Ellie's father hadn't heard this.

'Go and let the cat out, would you, please, Ellie? He sounds a bit desperate,' she heard him saying. Then he added into the phone, 'So you'd like one of us to pick her up? What time did you say?'

'Six?'

'Great!'

The doorbell rang again, and the potato water had now put out the gas flame completely. Lucy could smell gas already. Could she possibly stretch the phone cord far enough to reach the stove and—? No.

Meanwhile, Charlotte had bounced off into her room on the urgent mission of organising her toys ready for Ellie's visit.

'Oh, no! Too late! What a disaster!' Lucy heard at the other end of the phone. The final exclamation expressed her own sentiments rather nicely.

Clearly, neither harried parent wished to prolong this conversation. A minute later, she'd said a distracted goodbye, put down the phone, re-lit the gas and told the woman at the door that, thanks very much, she was *not* interested in glancing through her sales catalogue, either now or 'at her leisure' in order to have the opportunity of purchasing a range of innovative products at stunning value.

Two minutes after that, she'd caught her breath enough to realise that she still didn't know Ellie's last name, or her address, or the names of either of her parents. Not exactly the sort of parental vigilance she was happy with after only a month back in this city and with Charlotte less than two weeks into her school career.

Still, the whole thing seemed all right. Ellie's babysitter, Jenny, a woman in her early fifties, seemed caring and competent and nice. The little girl herself, too, just a tiny fairy of a thing, was obviously a well brought up and well cared for child.

Lucy sighed. She'd been a single mother for a long time. Effectively since Charlotte's conception, in fact. But living all of that time at her parents' farm with all their support and care had by no means prepared her for the inevitable reality of the new life she'd recently embarked on.

Changes happened, however, and in this case the changes were largely positive ones. Mum and Dad had made the reasoned decision that they were getting too old for the hard work of the farm. Dad didn't have the strength and stamina that he used to.

Lucy's older sister was happily married to a farmer and settled elsewhere, so there was no point in trying to keep the property in the family. Accordingly, Mum and Dad had sold it for a good price to a neighbour who was eager to expand his own holding. Then they'd made the big move from rural western New South Wales to a beachfront cottage in the pretty little town of Narrawallee on the south coast.

Their biggest concern at first had been Charlotte's and Lucy's future but, as Lucy had explained to them, she'd seen her own move away from the area, with her daughter, as increasingly inevitable over the past six months or so. Charlotte really was very bright and hungry to learn. At some stage in her future, she'd need far more than the local country schools could provide, and the move might as well be made now when she was young enough to adjust easily.

So here they were in Canberra, where Lucy had trained and worked as a nurse for several years, and Mum and Dad were less than three hours' drive away. She planned a weekend with them down at their new place very soon. Charlotte would love the sea, which she hadn't seen since she could remember.

But it wasn't the same as having her parents under the same roof, Lucy reflected. It would necessitate far more planning and efficiency on her part from now on.

And I haven't even started work yet. It's all going to get even more complicated after Monday…

Once dinner was on the table, then eaten and cleared away, however, Lucy was a little ashamed of her lack of courage. The summer evening was cooling nicely outside, thanks to a fresh breeze which came in a generous flow through the house's open windows. Charlotte was in the bath. There were some gorgeous salmon pink clouds banked high in the paling sky. Canberra had beautiful sunsets.

Lucy had a regular eight-till-four shift lined up in the accident and emergency department at nearby Black Mountain Hospital, starting Monday, which would mean that Charlotte could settle into a consistent routine of before and after school care at Lachlan Primary School, where she thus far appeared to be very happy, two weeks into the new school year. Mum and Dad had helped in the purchase of this very pleasant three-bedroom house just two minutes' drive from the school, and Charlotte already had a 'best friend' there, little Ellie. There was really very little to complain about.

And as long as Ellie's dad doesn't think back on our conversation, decide I must be far too scatterbrained to have his daughter under my supervision and cancel the whole arrangement...

Evidently he hadn't. The next afternoon at three, two little girls emerged from their classroom hand in hand, looking remarkably similar in their green cotton check uniform dresses, both with beaming smiles—smiles which must scarcely have left their faces for the next three hours, judging by the sounds emerging from the back garden, from Charlotte's room and from the dining room at snack time.

Apart from preparing the said snack and responding to a beseeching appeal for 'just one bucket of water in the garden for our game', Lucy herself was almost entirely superfluous to the girls' entertainment. This allowed her to finish painting a bookshelf in the living room, prepare a tuna casserole for dinner and go over once more the orientation material she'd been given by the hospital in preparation for starting her new job next week.

This time, when the doorbell rang at six, she wasn't on the phone, nothing was boiling over on the stove, and the girls were still happy in the back garden. She also knew it would be Ellie's father at the door, not an unwanted saleswoman with a catalogue.

It was hardly surprising, then, that she opened it confidently, ready to smile, invite him in and find out the trivial little detail of his name as soon as possible.

Not necessary, this last part, she found, when her stunned regard took in the details of the man on her doorstep. Tall. Dark. Grey-eyed. Dynamically built, yet with enormous sensitivity in his thirty-six-year-old face. Dressed in dark grey trousers and a pale grey shirt— conservative, well-tailored clothes that moulded easily to the body beneath. She knew his name already.

In fact, they each recognised the other at once. Six years really wasn't a long time. For Lucy, the shock was like a totally unexpected dousing with icy water. She felt an immediate, instinctive and quite unnecessary urge to protect herself physically by wrapping her arms across her chest or sheltering behind a piece of furniture, as if he represented a bodily danger.

For him…Malcolm…the reaction was apparently less intense. Or at least he was better at concealing it. After a moment of stunned silence, he was the one to recover his equilibrium and speak first.

'Lucy?' His voice betrayed just the tiniest note of huskiness. 'Lucy Beckett?' He searched her face for a moment, then stepped back a pace and glanced upwards at the house, as if it could instantly teach him more about her circumstances. 'Or…presumably it's not Beckett any more,' he amended.

'No, it's still Beckett,' she corrected quietly.

'Right. Right.' He swore mildly under his breath. 'But you *are* Charlotte's mother?'

'Yes. And, of course, it's Malcolm, isn't it?'

As if the issue was as casual as her words had sounded! And as if she was really in any doubt! He hadn't changed very much. She was simply buying time. For what, she didn't know. Nothing could over-come the impossible, uncomfortable reality of this meeting. My God, she'd cared for Charlotte's new best friend Ellie as tenderly as a mother when the tiny girl had been just a few weeks old!

Only her name hadn't been shortened back then. Dr Malcolm Lambert and his dying wife had called their newborn daughter Gabrielle.

'Come in,' Lucy managed, and they both stood awkwardly in the small, cream-painted hallway, then edged gradually into the living room. 'The girls are still playing out the back,' she went on, waving vaguely towards the windows that overlooked the garden. 'They've had a great time.'

'Yes, I could hear them from the driveway as I got out of the car,' Malcolm said.

He'd aged a little. Of course he had! Lucy could see it in the deepened etching of lines around his smoke-grey eyes and sensitively moulded mouth. At twenty-eight, and a mother for five years, she knew that she no longer looked as young and fresh as she once had either. And was her blouse still clean after cooking? Was it a crumpled mess? She smoothed it automatically, then forced her hands to be still. The convulsive movement betrayed far too much.

Malcolm went on, 'We'll give them a few minutes longer, shall we?'

'They're probably quite tired…'

'Oh, I expect so,' he agreed. 'They'll crash after dinner. Ellie has a tendency to subside in a sobbing heap after a long day, and school is wearing her out. But it's the weekend tomorrow after all.'

'True,' Lucy nodded. 'I've planned a quiet one for that same reason. I've learned the hard way that she's a horror if she doesn't get some time to unwind.'

'I expect it'll take a month or two before they get used to the pace. Fortunately, Ellie's babysitter seems well attuned to her needs.'

'You're lucky to have found her. She seems very

good. We got chatting the very first day, waiting to pick the girls up.'

Lord, we're both rambling! Lucy realised. They had moved as far as the windows that overlooked the back garden now, and could see that the two girls were still playing happily on the freshly mown grass.

It was a pretty sight. She'd had the sprinklers on last night and the lawn was green against the surrounding beds of summer flowers. Light shade from two tall birch trees saved the flowers from the worst stresses of the summer heat. Two blonde heads and two busy bodies, both in purple dresses, completed the picture. It seemed a shame to break it up…

Lucy wondered about offering Malcolm a drink, but decided that would only make things worse. What did you say in this situation? What did you *do*? She must be one of the last people in the world he'd ever have wanted to meet up with again, and as for how she felt about him… She couldn't even begin to think through the implications yet.

She felt sheer relief when he took control and brought things out into the open, speaking quietly and seriously. 'I'm sorry. We're both thinking of Bronwyn's death, aren't we? While trying very hard to pretend that we're not…'

'Yes.' She nodded, although it wasn't all she was thinking about. But Bronwyn's death was…well…the epicentre of the earthquake, if she wanted to be dramatic about it. 'It…wasn't an easy time,' she said inadequately. 'I—I'm sorry we had to meet again like this. I'm sure…that you don't want the memories made vivid again.'

It wasn't the first time she'd felt the need to spare him from torment.

'It was six years ago,' he answered. 'Just this time of year. February. The summer heat over Canberra brings it all back, no matter what else is going on in my life, but it does get a little easier each year. Please, don't feel you have to take responsibility for reviving my memories, Lucy. I'd hate to put that burden on you if our girls are going to be friends.'

His voice had that little husky note in it again. It had always shown what he'd felt.

'If?' she echoed on a laugh that wasn't quite steady. Who had the power to burden whom here? 'I'm getting the impression they're already joined at the hip!'

They both watched the girls again for a moment. Ellie's purple dress was far too big for her. It had been borrowed from Charlotte for the afternoon, as both girls had rejected the idea of remaining in their uniforms to play. They'd taken ages to choose alternatives, rummaging through Charlotte's entire wardrobe to find the nearest things to a matching pair of outfits.

I really must offer him a drink! Lucy decided. The house wasn't air-conditioned, and it was hot. Iced water was safe and appropriate, surely? He accepted the suggestion, and they both stood there, making their tall glasses tinkle with the movement of the ice as they drank. Somehow, it seemed only natural to stand close together as they watched their daughters. She felt her pale green skirt drag a little against his leg.

'I'm delighted about it, actually,' Malcolm said, picking up the conversation from where it had left off a few minutes previously. 'Their friendship,' he clarified unnecessarily. 'I worried a lot about Ellie starting school. In fact, she could have started last year if I'd wanted her to, being a January baby and already six now, but I kept her back a year in the hope that she'd look a little less small and delicate. I didn't want her to get teased. But even this year, with her classmates a good year or more younger in many cases, she's still quite a bit smaller. Your Charlotte, for example, looks like such a strong, sturdy lass by comparison.'

'Fortunately, I don't think children form friendships on the basis of size,' Lucy said with a laugh.

'No, I guess they don't,' he agreed. 'I do tend to be over-protective. A symptom of single parenthood, perhaps.'

'Perhaps.' She nodded, then added reluctantly, although he'd probably guessed after what she'd said about her last name, 'I'm a single parent, too.'

There was a tiny silence while they watched the girls again. There was an elaborate role-playing game going on, involving dolls and toy animals and a large shrub at the edge of the lawn. Glancing sideways, Lucy could see how closely Malcolm's gaze followed his daughter's movements. Those lashes of his were as long and thick as she remembered. She had to look away quickly when he turned to focus on her instead.

'Fill me in a bit, Lucy,' he said. His interest seemed polite. He was going through the motions. If there was any passion lying below the surface, he was concealing it. And yet there was no way of talking about her life without stripping away the layers and getting personal straight away. 'You were planning to go overseas…' he prompted.

'Didn't happen.' She smiled.

There were no regrets. That was the thing about having a child come into your life. Charlotte's unexpected conception had changed everything about Lucy's plans, and yet there hadn't been a moment of real regret. She loved Charlotte with all her heart.

'After I... Well, after Bronwyn's death,' she went on, 'when I stopped working for you, I went back to my parents' farm. It was meant to be a short stay before my friend was ready to set off on our big trip, but I...' She hesitated. So many people to protect with the shield of some simple words. They had to be well chosen. 'I met someone.'

'The old story, I suppose,' he supplied helpfully.

'Exactly! It didn't last long, though. When he found out that Charlotte was on the way, he ran a mile.'

She was well aware that she was over-simplifying the facts hugely, to the point of untruth, but it seemed necessary, as it had seemed necessary for years.

'That must have been hard,' he said.

'I don't blame him,' she replied truthfully. 'He was only twenty-one.'

'Not ready for fatherhood,' Malcolm conceded. 'Yet you were about the same age, surely?'

'Twenty-two,' she confirmed. 'But I think girls... young women...can often be more mature. Even if only because they're forced to be! But, anyway, I had my parents.'

Who had been fantastic from the word go. Supportive both emotionally and practically. Never asking too many questions. And best of all, perhaps, resisting any temptation to try and railroad Brett into 'doing the right thing'. Because, even at the time, she'd known without a shadow of a doubt that it wouldn't have been the right thing at all.

'After Charlotte was born, I was able to start nursing in Casualty at the local hospital, with Mum and Dad's help,' she went on quickly. 'So I didn't lose ground professionally.'

'And now you're back in Canberra,' Malcolm finished for her.

'Yes.'

She quickly sketched her reasons for the move, while wondering in the back of her mind whether she'd have chosen this city, this hospital—the house was set high up and she could actually glimpse the eight-storey main hospital building in the distance, above the grey-green of its surrounding eucalpytus trees—if she'd had the remotest reason to suspect Malcolm would be here, too.

She hadn't forgotten that he'd been working in emergency medicine six years ago...

'And what about you?' she added. It came out abruptly, almost like an accusation. Perhaps it *was* one. *Why* was he here? He'd moved to Brisbane not long after Bronwyn's death, she was sure of it. He'd certainly been planning to. Why had he come back?

The explanation turned out to be simple, and contained the news she feared.

'I spent nearly three years in Brisbane,' he said, 'but the climate wasn't great for Ellie. Even with air-conditioning she wilted in the heat and humidity up there, and lost her appetite on hot, sticky days, which she couldn't afford to do. Three years ago, we came back here for a friend's wedding in late March, when it was still stinking hot in Brisbane.

'We took a two-week break here and the difference in Ellie's energy levels on those crisp, sunny Canberra autumn days was just so marked that I couldn't ignore it. I grew up in Canberra. I'd always liked the place, till the shadow of Bronwyn's illness fell over it, and for my daughter's sake the move back seemed right. I took up basically the same position as I'd had before, in the accident and emergency department at Black Mountain Hospital, only at a more senior level.'

'Right.' The news thudded into Lucy's consciousness entirely unaccompanied by surprise, and she informed him as neutrally as she could, 'We'll meet up, then. A lot. I work in emergency medicine now, too. I start at Black Mountain on Monday.'

Before he could react, they both heard the back screen door crash open and two pairs of sneaker-clad feet—surely belonging to an elephant, not two little girls—thundered inside.

'We're *starving*!' Charlotte announced. 'Can we have some more to eat?'

'No, love,' Lucy said. 'It's dinnertime, not snack-time, and Ellie's dad is here to take her home.'

'Oh…' Charlotte whined in protest, while Ellie gave a graphic sigh.

'Hi, Daddy…' Her tone was one of weary resignation, as if to suggest that parents were *always* turning up to spoil the fun and children were absolute saints to put up with it.

'Glad you missed me, sunshine,' Malcolm drawled, and his grey eyes met Lucy's green ones. The two girls didn't see the shared smile—a smile that shot straight to Lucy's heart.

'I'm not trying to hurt your feelings, Daddy, but—' Ellie began.

'Couldn't they stay to dinner, Mummy?' Charlotte interrupted. Both girls clearly considered the idea in-spirational.

Their parents didn't agree. There was another silent meeting of looks, communicating this time a whole, complex and very adult repertoire of attitudes—polite regret, acknowledgement of the immutability of plans and a tentative willingness to consider the idea some other time. But definitely not now.

'No, love,' both Lucy and Malcolm said to their respective daughters in unison. 'Not today.'

'But why *not*?'

Why indeed?

'Because you're both tired,' Lucy said truthfully.

Malcolm supplied, with a little more cunning, 'Because Charlotte's mum only has enough dinner for two.'

Negotiations could have gone on for a lot longer. Lucy was rather surprised that they didn't. Clearly, beneath their exuberance, the girls really *were* tired. They contented themselves with extracting a tentative commitment from each adult to make it 'another time' and didn't even press home their advantage by insisting on a fixed date.

It took a further five minutes to locate Ellie's discarded shoes, uniform, backpack and school hat and argue politely over whether or not Malcolm would wash the purple dress before giving it back. Then, to Lucy's inexpressible relief, they were gone.

She had her thoughts to herself. She didn't have to pretend—or only to Charlotte, who was too tired and absorbed in her own life to notice her mother's preoccupation. Lucy would have a chance to work out how much this collision with the past really mattered.

Because, of course, she'd been in love with Malcolm Lambert six years ago. So terribly, impossibly in love that even now the memory of it was painful and the sight and sound of him, during those ten minutes they'd just spent together, deeply disturbing. They'd lived under the same roof for nearly four months. She had so many memories of him to relive on seeing him again. He was so familiar.

And after Charlotte was in bed that night, conking out, as expected, on the dot of seven-thirty, Lucy had the whole evening to herself to think about it...

Malcolm himself had spoken this afternoon about the way seasons triggered memories. As he'd said, the last stage of Bronwyn Lambert's long dying had taken place here in Canberra in the hot month of February, when dry, shimmering heat over several days could then build into dramatic evening thunderstorms, signalled by heaps of billowing grey-purple cloud massing over the sprawling, tree-filled city.

Bronwyn had suffered in the heat all through that summer, but she'd insisted on remaining at home. Strong-willed and absorbed by her own illness, she hadn't been an easy patient. But, then, why should she have been? She'd been thirty-one years old, pregnant with her first child, and dying of breast cancer.

There had been many days when Bronwyn's stubbornness and temper might have driven Lucy to abandon her position as the Lamberts' private nurse, if it hadn't been for the heart-wrenching poignancy of their situation.

Lucy had never intended to go into private nursing. She and a friend, Angie, had been planning a two-year working holiday overseas, and both had actually resigned from their positions at Canberra Hospital when family commitments had forced Angie to delay her trip by several months. Lucy hadn't wanted to depart alone, so she'd delayed hers, too, deciding to make good use of the time by working as an agency nurse. She'd gone to work for the Lamberts in early November.

By then, Bronwyn had already made the impossible decision which had very possibly cost her her life. Lucy knew it had been Bronwyn's decision, not Malcolm's, to refuse treatment for her cancer in order to continue safely with her pregnancy. Bronwyn herself had been very clear about that.

'*I* wanted it this way! And I'm *not* going to admit defeat! I'll have my baby *and* my life!'

She kept on saying this when everyone else, including Malcolm, knew that there was no hope. Lucy suspected there were some terrible fights between the two of them. They were both strong people.

Seeing the anguish in Malcolm's face day after day, she began to share his suffering more and more. She didn't, then, have the slightest idea about the real depth of her feelings, or what they meant. She thought right until the end that it was purely empathy for his situation.

Time passed. During the Christmas season, the Lamberts and Bronwyn's doctors agonised over how long to let the pregnancy continue. At first, Bronwyn was the one to argue passionately for waiting longer.

'I *won't* risk my baby's health and life by inducing her too early!'

Then, abruptly, in the middle of January, she changed her mind, and it was, at last, an acceptance of the inevitable. 'I want to be with her, know her just a little, before it's too late.'

They admitted her to Black Mountain Hospital and induced labour on 16 January, at thirty-four weeks' gestation. On the 26th, both mother and baby were ready to come home, with Lucy's continued attendance. For four weeks, she and Malcolm both worked themselves into the ground to fulfil the very different needs of a terminally ill mother and her fragile new baby.

Lucy still vividly remembered the ragged nights, the baby's cries, the constant fight to adjust Bronwyn's pain medication and the moments when she and Malcolm would meet in the kitchen at some unholy pre-dawn hour and sit in exhausted silence over hot chocolate or coffee.

Then, on 28 February, Bronwyn Lambert finally gave up her fight.

Five days later, an exhausted, grief- and guilt-stricken Malcolm Lambert told Lucy that she should leave, in torn, incoherent sentences which, too, she could still remember with painful clarity, just as she could remember her own responses.

'What sort of a man am I?' His head, with dark, unkempt hair that looked as if it hadn't been brushed in days, was buried in his hands. 'I should have done everything differently. I love my daughter, but should I have let my wife sacrifice her own life so that Gabrielle could be born?'

'Malcolm, you didn't have a choice,' Lucy answered urgently, racked by the inadequacy of her own power to help him. She ached to touch him. Just a squeeze of his hand or a press of his shoulder, but even that was out of the question. Especially now. Oh, Lord, especially now! 'Bronwyn would never have consented—'

'I could have argued harder! Did I love her enough, I wonder? Perhaps I didn't. I can't have, if—'

'Malcolm—'

'Don't! Don't take any notice.' His burning storm-grey eyes swept upwards to fix on her, then closed as he covered them once more with his hands. 'It's not your problem. It's not your fault. *None* of this is your problem. You know that, don't you?' There was a white-hot urgency to the question.

'I—'

'I'm planning to leave Canberra as soon as I can,' he went on, not waiting for her answer, thank goodness.

'There's a job in Brisbane. Lucy, Gabrielle doesn't need a trained nurse any more, and after—'

'I can't stay. I know that,' she agreed quickly, before he could finish. 'My God! The last thing I want is for you to think I was expecting to *stay*!'

'I've already arranged my resignation from the hospital,' he told her. 'I'll care for Gabrielle myself until we're settled in Brisbane. Please, leave as soon as you want to.'

And as it was quite unbearable to stay, she packed her things and said goodbye to Gabrielle and Malcolm that same day…only to realise then, finally, as she travelled the long hours to her parents' farm, that the reason she ached so badly for Malcolm, with all that had happened, wasn't simply out of sympathy for what he'd been through.

It was because she loved him.

In hindsight, it wasn't very fair to Brett, a young motor mechanic from Brewarra, the modest-sized town nearest her parents' farm. She went out with him on the rebound, only it felt far more desperate and confusing and *necessary* at the time than that shallow phrase could express. She wasn't using him. But their relationship could never have worked in the long term, and she could hardly blame him for wanting no part of Charlotte's future.

So there it was. The most painful, turbulent period of her life—and, no doubt, of Malcolm Lambert's as well—and by returning to Canberra she'd walked right back into her memories of it, like walking into a brick wall in the dark, because she hadn't even considered that he'd have had any reason to come back here himself.

'And our daughters are best friends,' she whispered aloud at ten o'clock as she climbed, wrung out, into her solitary bed. 'Just how impossible is this going to be?'

CHAPTER TWO

'I KNOW I'm not the man you want to hear from at four o'clock on a Sunday afternoon,' said Matt Grady at the other end of the phone.

'It's not a social call, then?' Malcolm answered. He had known Matt for years, and the two of them now held equivalent positions, Matt at a regional hospital in a nearby country town and Malcolm at Canberra's largest hospital.

'I don't make social calls,' Matt replied. 'My wife makes those! No, but don't get too alarmed. I'm putting you on the alert just in case. We've got a report from the State Emergency Service of a big bushfire around Tumut, with probable casualties coming in. One volunteer firefighter is already on his way to us with facial burns and smoke inhalation. The fire's still out of control, with no change forecast until tomorrow, so the S.E.S. says we can expect some drama for at least the next forty-eight hours.'

'You'll be the first port of call for casualties, presumably?' Malcolm guessed. 'Since you're closer to the action.'

'Yes, but we're not well set up to deal with burns or major trauma,' Matt answered.

'What about Westmead?' Malcolm asked, naming the large hospital in Sydney's west end which received serious injuries flown in from a wide catchment area.

'Preferably not,' Matt answered. 'There are more fires

in the Blue Mountains and they're expecting to be squeezed pretty tightly with those.'

'Then—'

'As I said, don't react too strongly at this stage. For now, loll by the pool, spoil your lady-friend and keep those peeled grapes coming, but your department may get roped in to this later.'

'OK, thanks for letting me know, Matt.' Malcolm closed up his mobile phone and put it back in the canvas beach bag that sat on the picnic table in front of him.

Then he smiled. Matt had been joking, and there were no peeled grapes in the picture, but he was, in fact, lolling by the pool and spoiling his lady-friend.

Well, his daughter, actually, but they *were* friends, he considered, and he was proud of their relationship. It was easily the most important thing in his life.

He watched Ellie for a moment as she made serious inroads into her chocolate ice cream. There was a sticky brown tideline all around her mouth now, the ice cream was melting fast and she was having to concentrate hard in order to get each piece of chocolate coating safely into her mouth before it slid off the creamy part beneath and dropped to the ground. Malcolm didn't have the tidemark, but he was having a similar struggle with his own chocolate bits now. They'd got a head start on melting while his mouth had been out of action on the phone.

They'd had a nice weekend together, he and Ellie. Quiet. Technically, as Matt Grady's phone call had just proved, he was on call all the time as head of Black Mountain Hospital's Accident and Emergency Department, but, in fact, a call like Matt's was a rare event, and most of his weeks involved regular hours,

Monday to Friday from eight until six, with the occasional overnight to cover gaps in the roster.

Ellie's babysitter, Jenny, was almost always available to stay over on those occasions, and if by chance she wasn't, she had a grown up daughter, Clare, studying at university, whom Ellie liked—and he trusted—almost as much, and who was happy to fill in.

Ellie slid the wooden ice-cream stick between her lips to remove the last of the chocolate goo, then did it again just to make absolutely sure that she wasn't missing a bit. Then she inspected it very seriously.

'Are you keeping it?' he asked her, knowing the answer would be yes. At home, she had a plastic takeaway food container almost full of them now, destined for some as yet undetermined on but very important craft project. 'Here…'

He took it from her and put it in a side pocket of the canvas bag, then wiped the chocolate from her face with a small cloth brought for that purpose. Ice cream was a regular feature of their frequent swims at the local outdoor heated public pool.

Was it a little shocking that Ellie had *so* many ice-cream sticks in her collection, though? He felt a moment's twinge of guilt, then let it go. He loved to watch Ellie eat, and in general he was careful about the make-up of her diet. He got an active pleasure from seeing her relishing her food and taking something like an ice cream so seriously. She'd been so very delicate as a baby.

Inevitably, he found himself thinking of Lucy Beckett and their startling meeting, out of the blue, on Friday. Ellie's health, his love for his child, Lucy's role in his life, grief and guilt… It was all tangled up together. The grief was perhaps the least of it now. As he'd told

Lucy, year by year for six years Bronwyn's loss had become a little less acute. ·

He'd certainly battled with it at the beginning, though…

'Are we having another swim, Daddy?' Ellie wanted to know.

'Are you all warmed up?'

'Yes.' She nodded firmly.

With so little padding on her bones, she felt the cold, but usually refused to emerge from the water until her lips were purple and her teeth chattering…only to turn, with no sense of incongruity, to filling her stomach with an ice-cold treat.

'OK, then, another swim,' he conceded. 'But I won't come in the water this time, possum.'

There was a large shadecloth-covered children's pool, where Ellie was well within her depth and quite safe as she splashed about and practised her sketchy swimming strokes.

'OK, Daddy. Do you have to ring the hospital?' She always associated his mobile phone with the demands of his work.

'No, I have to ring Jenny. I'm going to ask her to stay the night in case I have to go in to the hospital later.'

'Is someone hurt?'

'Some people might be, some time. They're fighting a big bushfire. We'll hope they're all OK, though.'

'Yes,' she agreed easily, and they walked along the cement path back to the children's pool with no further comment from her on the subject. She was splashing her way into the middle of the pool seconds later.

Malcolm didn't like her to dwell on the harsher re-alities of his work. In fact, he actively protected her from such things, and he often envied her her youthful ability to live in the moment. He was grateful, too, for the fact that she forced *him* to do so as well. In the months following Bronwyn's death, caring for Ellie was possibly the only thing that had kept him sane.

He was definitely thinking about it all much more this weekend, after seeing Lucy…

She, too, had been one of the vital factors in keeping him going six years ago, until he'd so abruptly sent her away. It hadn't even occurred to him until afterwards how cruel that might have been. To do it so suddenly when she'd already been so attached to Ellie. It had been typical of her maturity, her generosity and her sense of honour, he considered, that she'd agreed so quickly to what he'd asked and had made her departure so smooth and unfussed.

But, then, honourable as she'd been, perhaps she'd been as tormented by guilt and regret as he'd been, and had been just as anxious to be free of his presence.

They'd slept together.

Even now, he couldn't fully understand how it had happened. 'Slept together' wasn't right, anyway. What an inaccurate euphemism that could be! There had been no *sleep* involved during that single, impossible episode. No real *togetherness*, either. They'd actually been far closer, emotionally and in spirit, at other times during Lucy's period of employment as Bronwyn's nurse. Still, it had been the physical thing that had felt like the betrayal.

It had happened just four days after Bronwyn's death, at the point where the engine of nervous energy that had kept him going for months through Bronwyn's pregnancy and illness, and through the funeral and various other practical arrangements, had finally run down, leaving him totally empty, totally vulnerable.

Stupidly, and not in character at all, he'd turned to alcohol. Not enough to knock himself out, unfortunately, just enough to completely impair his judgement and his control.

He remembered talking to Lucy in the kitchen—imprisoning her there, really, with his slurred, repetitive, anguished words—then saying goodnight to her. It must have been well after midnight. She'd gone along to her room to get ready for bed. He had… He couldn't remember what he'd done at this point…

Then they'd both met outside baby Gabrielle's room some minutes later, intending to check on her, and somehow…perhaps it was better that he couldn't remember…he'd taken her into his arms and ravished her with clumsy, desperate kisses…kisses which had soon led on, beyond control, to a feverish interlude of lovemaking—another inaccurate euphemism—on the hall carpet.

The release of tension, the brief immersion in another universe of fabulous sensation, had been incredible for both of them. Immediately afterwards, however, she'd gasped out something he hadn't understood and had fled into her room. He hadn't seen her again that night.

He'd gritted his teeth for the task, and had asked her to leave the next day.

And she had. And now that he knew about Charlotte he felt to blame for that, too. Lucy had only been twenty-two. She'd nursed both Bronwyn and the baby with such tireless tenderness and commitment. He didn't know why she'd initially accepted his lovemaking that night. It could only be, surely, that she'd felt sorry for him.

But it must have confused the hell out of her! She wasn't the type that slept around, and he was eight years older, the one who should have been in control. So she'd fled home and rebounded into some doomed relationship with a local boy, and Charlotte was the result.

Yes, he could be in great danger of feeling very responsible for Charlotte's existence. And this at a point in his life where he'd been sure that he'd resolved all the issues of grief and guilt connected with Bronwyn's death a long time ago.

He hadn't resolved them alone. He'd had a close friend, Adam, who'd been training for the Anglican priesthood at the time, and Adam had helped to an incalculable degree. After hours of Adam's constructive listening on many occasions over several months, Malcolm had felt so—to use a current buzzword—*healed*. So at peace with himself about all that had happened, in fact, that when he'd first seen Lucy at her front door on Friday evening, as neat and attractive as ever in a pale green summery cotton skirt and a matching top, and had realised who she was, he'd felt more pleasure than anything else.

So Ellie's new best friend's mother was someone he knew and trusted! Marvellous! You had to be careful these days, and their phone conversation the day before had been impossible. He'd been somewhat concerned at knowing so little about where his daughter had been spending the afternoon. And it had been good to see how well Lucy Beckett was doing for herself, too. A pleasant house, a bright, healthy child…and a face and figure only a little changed in six years.

Oddly, Bronwyn had been the one, six years ago, to point out just how attractive Lucy Beckett had been. Many women might not have done so, but Bronwyn had always possessed such driving confidence in herself that it would never have occurred to her that it might have been dangerous to draw her husband's attention to another woman's charms.

'And it wasn't just confidence in herself,' Malcolm remembered, speaking the words under his breath. 'She had confidence in me, too. She made me believe in myself when we first got together at university years earlier, after that lonely, over-sheltered childhood of mine, in a way I'd never done before. That was one of the reasons I loved her…'

Bronwyn's confidence and her strong convictions, the most powerful features of her emotional make-up.

'How terrific to have a really nice-looking nurse!' she'd said to Malcolm after they'd interviewed several candidates, chosen Lucy and had experienced her sunny efficiency and care for over a week. 'I'll tell her so when this is all over. Lovely trim, graceful figure. *Beautiful* green eyes. Really warm, sweet smile.'

'Yes, she does, doesn't she?'

'Her hair, too. It's only that insipid pale mousy brown, so it could be awful, except that she keeps it so clean and silky and bouncing, and tricks it up into all those pretty, imaginative styles with clips and combs and so forth. So far I don't think she's worn the same one twice, and it really looks nice. Don't you think, Mal? Don't you think it's going to help enormously in me keeping a positive attitude to have someone pretty and bright like Lucy around me all day long?'

There was a plaintive, fatigued and slightly desperate note to this last question. Bronwyn was losing strength and focus daily.

'Definitely,' he agreed, hiding his doubt—not about

Lucy's prettiness, but about the power of it to do Bronwyn any good.

'We must tell her not to bother with a uniform,' Bronwyn decided with her usual authority. 'I'd much rather see her in nice colours and softer styles. Wouldn't you?'

'It's up to you, Bronny.'

'Well, I would.'

So, after the second week, Lucy didn't wear a uniform, and Bronwyn had been right. Lucy's own clothing suited her far better, and she always looked fresh and nice.

'And if I hadn't been so concerned with Bronwyn and the baby, perhaps I'd have sensed that there was danger, that I had the capacity to find her attractive. Hell, I didn't think I had a particle of sensuality left in me then! If I'd seen it coming, *remotely* seen it coming, maybe I wouldn't have cracked that night...'

It was impossible and useless to conjecture on the subject. He could never truly know. And, until Friday, it had ceased to matter. It had been in the past.

Now, however...

He spent a few pointless moments rewriting reality. If Lucy could have found the *right* man to be Charlotte's father. If he'd encountered her on her doorstep on Friday evening as a happily married woman, then it would all be easy, wouldn't it?

At the heart of his complicated feelings about Lucy was simple gratitude—gratitude that she'd done so much to ease Bronwyn's death and dying, and to nurture Ellie's fragile new life. Gratitude that, whatever she'd felt that night in his arms, she'd somehow understood enough of what *he'd* felt to take herself out of his life with no drama.

If she'd been married to Charlotte's father, he could have evolved a casual sort of friendship with both Lucy and her husband, based on their daughters' friendship. As the situation stood, however, and with the prospect of seeing her frequently at work, he had the strong intuition that it wasn't going to be so easy.

'Look at me going underwater, Daddy!' Ellie commanded, then ducked beneath the water and held her breath for a whole five seconds.

'Fabulous!' Malcolm told her. 'You're getting so brave about that now. Remember last summer when you wouldn't do it at all?'

'I'd only turned *five* last summer,' she answered, scorning her younger self.

Malcolm hid a smile, and felt his priorities shift back into place. Ellie mattered. And if Lucy was going to matter in future, it would be as the mother of Ellie's friend. If he kept that fact in view, then neither of them…none of them…had anything to worry about.

Taking his mobile out of the beach bag, he dialled Jenny Boyd's phone number.

'Normally, you'd get a better orientation than this on your first day,' Malcolm apologised hurriedly to Lucy the following Monday morning at eight-fifteen.

He looked tired, the phone on his cluttered desk was ringing, and already there was a junior doctor in the doorway, anxious for his presence at a patient's bedside. It was typical of the man, Lucy considered, that he hadn't mentioned on Friday that he was, in fact, the head of this entire department.

He had over forty medical and administrative staff under his supervision, rotating to cover the full twenty-four hours, seven days a week. His department was the first port of call in any emergency, major or minor. Ultimately, when patients died here, as inevitably they sometimes did, he was the one who had to ask himself whether he and his staff had done everything they could.

'Dr Lambert…?'

'I'm coming,' he promised the young doctor.

'Look, I know about the bushfires,' Lucy told him.

'It's not only the fires, unfortunately,' he explained. 'There's been a serious crash involving a minibus and a van, and we've got another patient who's arrested twice in the past half-hour. I've been in here since two a.m. Look, I'm going to put you in the cubes and free up someone else to work the trolleys for today,' he went on quickly. 'If things get quiet, go over to Personnel, as you're supposed to do, and fill in all the forms and so forth, but meanwhile I just can't spare you—I'm sorry—and Personnel will have to lump it.'

'The cubes…'

'Non-urgent cubicles. Normally, given your experience, you won't be doing those, but as yet, since you don't know our procedures, our staff—'

'It's fine, Dr Lambert.'

'Malcolm, for heaven's sake!'

The sudden impatience in his tone told Lucy he really didn't have time to prolong this, so she repeated his first name quickly, suppressing her awareness of the memories it brought, then stood up and headed for the door. Before reaching it, she stepped aside to let him and Dr Brian Smith hurry through ahead of her.

They turned right, and ahead of them she heard the urgent voices of medical staff gathered around the patient who'd arrested. They were trying to shock his heart back into life with a defibrillator, and the scene was stark and shocking. A naked chest jumped and fell back each time the current pulsed through the twin paddles of the machine.

Turning left, she made the correct assumption that she was heading in the direction of 'the cubes'.

It meant that she wouldn't see much of Malcolm today. In his position as head of department, he would only oversee the non-urgent cases in the most general way. Much of his time would be taken up with administration, paperwork and liaison with other parts of the hospital, and his practice of medicine would be limited to the true emergencies—those patients who occupied the 'trolleys' in the high-tech, open area at the far end of the department.

Cardiac arrests would command his attention if the more junior doctors, training as emergency specialists, needed his help. Also, he'd see acute asthma attacks, serious road trauma injuries, severe unexplained pain, dangerous bleeding, life-threatening overdoses…

All the cases, in other words, which needed urgent stabilisation before they could be admitted to the relevant ward or sent for emergency surgery. But he wouldn't see the sort of 'GP cases', as they were sometimes known, which she would be dealing with today.

Perhaps it would help to have this first day to orientate herself without the added complication of his presence.

She'd had the weekend to think about it, and had basically found that nothing in her attitude to Malcolm Lambert and what he represented had changed in the past six years. She'd always known exactly how appalled and guilty Malcolm had felt about that one desperate eruption of passion between them. Now, as then, she was going to do all she could to protect him from the need to relive it, dwell on it, bring it into the present.

There *was* no need! Who would benefit after all this time? No one! Things were best left as they were. Dismissing the subject, and hoping for the sort of day that would keep her mind busy and her hands filled, she focused on work instead.

It was a little strange to be working at a large facility like this again after her years at Brewarra Base Hospital in far western New South Wales. They dealt with plenty of emergencies in Brewarra, but not all at once, and things weren't so strictly divided into urgent and non-urgent cases there.

Brewarra Base Hospital had no triage nurse to prioritise the treatment of each patient, and its staff turned back and forth between an acute asthma attack, a peanut up a toddler's nose and a major heart attack in the same way that the owner of the town's sprawling and eclectic general store turned back and forth between selling a chocolate bar and selling a ride-on lawnmower.

Here, the set-up was a little more intimidating. The hospital was modern and well equipped, and staff, as much as patients, ran the gamut of human personalities.

For the next two hours, as she'd hoped, Lucy didn't have time to think about Malcolm. There was a steady stream of Monday morning patients—those who'd done something to themselves on the weekend and had decided overnight that perhaps it really did need treatment, those who'd left it too late to get an appointment with their GP today and those who'd partied hard on the weekend and had been too tired to avoid careless accidents as a result.

Lucy dressed some minor lacerations, made an old lady comfortable while she was waiting for the doctor, took some blood and gave a local anaesthetic. She comforted a crying young woman, distracted a toddler while his ear was syringed, did a pregnancy test and took numerous blood pressures and pulses.

It was routine, familiar work, and work that she enjoyed. Time always seemed to pass quickly when there was one thing after another like this, and when every patient was so different. The stoics and the complainers, the demanding and the docile, the chronically ill and the 'never needed a doctor before in my life' types. You had to be a student of human nature to get the most out of nursing.

With several people she shared a laugh, with a couple more she listened to problems which had nothing to do with the medical issue that had brought them in. And once she almost cried.

'Everything was normal. I was at work,' the thirty-eight-year-old woman said tearfully. 'I felt some cramping pains and I went to the bathroom. I thought it was a stomach upset. But then I just started to bleed.'

'Are you here on your own?' Lucy asked. The patient was shaking and very upset as she lay back on the examining bench in one of the cubicles.

'Yes. A friend from the office drove me, but she had an important meeting to get back to and I told her to go. My husband's away until tomorrow. *Is* it a miscarriage?'

'It may very well be,' Lucy had to say. 'The doctor should be here any minute to examine you properly. If you could take off your lower clothing and lie down. Here's a sheet to put over you.'

She left the room for a few minutes to give the patient her privacy, then entered again in the wake of second-year resident Andrew Carter. He seemed like a good and caring doctor, pleasant in manner, freckle-faced, quite good-looking, but ultimately powerless to ease this situation for his patient.

Reaching his gloved hand beneath the sheet, he did an internal examination and Jill Lewis winced and tensed and held her breath. 'Just try to relax, Mrs Lewis,' he murmured, and she nodded and began to take deep breaths instead as he felt her cervix.

It didn't take long before he announced quietly, 'Your cervix has opened to three centimetres.'

'What does that—?'

'Well, not good news, I'm afraid, and the cramping isn't a good sign. Was this your first pregnancy?'

'Yes. And I knew it was too good to be true,' she said bitterly. 'We'd almost given up hope. I'd rather not have got pregnant at all than had that false joy two weeks ago when I did the test, and then this.'

'So you hadn't seen anyone for your antenatal care yet?' Dr Carter clarified gently.

'Not yet,' Jill Lewis answered. 'I'd made an appointment with the antenatal clinic, though. I'll have to cancel it...'

'We'll send you over to Pathology, and they'll take some blood to be tested for the levels of pregnancy hormone, just to make sure.'

'OK.' She nodded, while Dr Carter quickly scrawled on the necessary form. A minute later, he'd left to see the next waiting patient.

'Do I just get dressed now?' Mrs Lewis asked tonelessly.

'You don't have to,' Lucy answered, 'if you'd like to rest a little first. Shall I bring you a cup of tea?'

'Yes, please. I'm sorry I'm upset,' she apologised, and tried to pull herself together.

Lucy wanted to tell her, 'Don't! You needn't be afraid to cry and let it out.' Instead, she just patted Mrs Lewis on the shoulder silently.

'Do you have any children?' Mrs Lewis asked suddenly, just as Lucy was about to leave.

'A daughter. She's five.'

'You don't know how lucky you are.' She began to cry again.

Yes, I do, Lucy thought as she went to get the patient's tea. She swallowed against a lump in her throat and blinked twice as her eyes brimmed. I *do* know exactly how lucky I am!

At eleven there was a lull, and Kerry Anderson, who headed up the nursing side of the team, told her, 'Go over to Personnel *now* before we get busy again and I tell you that you can't. Thanks for jumping in the way you did.'

'It hasn't been hard,' Lucy answered. 'Are you still busy down the far end?'

An ambulance siren at that moment saved Kerry from having to answer the question and both women pulled faces.

'Did you feel that hot north wind this morning?' Kerry said. 'Worst weather for fires. But the change is due through late this afternoon from the south-west, with rain.'

'Thank goodness! Although the season isn't over yet.'

'We're always at the mercy of the climate in this country, aren't we?'

'You don't have to tell me! I'm a farmer's daughter.'

It took two hours to go through all the formalities that Personnel dictated to be necessary, and Lucy was finally free for a late lunch, which she ate quickly in the staff cafeteria, sitting alone as she tried to collate her first impressions. It hadn't been a typical day so far, but the signs were good, and there was that subtle, indefinable sense that the accident and emergency department was a happy one, and ran smoothly.

She wasn't surprised, since it had Malcolm Lambert at its head. He was the kind of man who knew when his staff were happy, and cared if they weren't.

He'd even found time to care today, she found a moment later as his shadow fell over her table and he pulled up a chair to sit down. 'Did Personnel terrorise you with forms?' he asked.

'A bit. And I'd forgotten to bring my tax file number.'

'You bad person!'

'I know. I have a mental block about my tax file number. Would a sensible person commit it to memory?'

'I've asked myself the same question in the past. I can reel off the first three digits of it, but somehow, to people who concern themselves with such things, that's never enough, and they want the whole nine.'

'Good heavens! How petty of them!' she teased.

'I know. Like us boring medical people insisting on knowing *exactly* what prescription medicine someone is taking, not just that it's ''something for my heart''. But, seriously, no problems so far?'

'None,' she answered him truthfully. 'It's a lovely hospital, isn't it?' she went on, perhaps too quickly. 'The setting, I mean. All surrounded by trees and wild bushland, yet so close to the centre of the city.'

'The only thing I regret about having chosen to work in emergency medicine,' he answered, 'is that A and E departments are always on the ground floor.'

'I think there's a reason for that,' she dared to tease again.

'I know.' He laughed. 'But every now and then I do envy obstetricians and cardiologists and renal specialists, who get to stroll around on the upper floors when they do their rounds and take in that glorious view of the surrounding trees and the mountains to the west through the windows of every ward.'

They'd always been able to talk easily like this, Lucy remembered as he got up to leave a few minutes later. He'd eaten hungrily and fast—she suspected this was breakfast as well as lunch for him today—and hadn't slowed himself down with tea or coffee. He'd insisted that she do so, however, so she had time to think after he'd gone.

Which wasn't, perhaps, a good thing. She thought about *him*, and all those times six years ago when they'd sat quietly together over meals. She realised only now, for the first time, just how strong a foundation they'd laid, during those times, for what had happened afterwards. She realised, too, how little either of them had understood about the danger.

And she wondered if it would have happened if Malcolm hadn't been drinking. She wondered if it would have happened if she'd realised earlier that she'd been in love with him then.

They'd been standing outside Gabrielle's—Ellie's—door. There had been a nightlight plugged into a power outlet in the hall at ankle level, giving the thickly carpeted space a dim golden glow. He'd smelled—not unpleasantly—of the red wine he'd been drinking, and she'd already made a mental note to herself: headache tablets and B vitamins and lots of fluids for him in the morning.

Her heart had ached for him so badly. Perhaps that had been why she hadn't guessed much sooner how she'd truly felt. She'd had such overwhelming reasons for sympathy that she'd thought that was all it had been.

Even standing there, watching in some alarm as he'd lurched against the wall of the corridor to shore himself up and given a hiccup that had been far more like a sob, and feeling her hands literally ache and itch to reach up and smooth the unkempt dark hair from his forehead, or massage the lines of tension and pain from his face, she'd thought of her touch on his skin purely as healing, not as sensual.

She even started to lift her hand. Somehow, they were standing very close. She could have reached him without moving. Did that mean that *she* was the one to initiate what happened? Unconsciously, with just that one tentative and uncompleted gesture?

Because her hand never got as far as his forehead. Instead, a second later, it was crushed between her chest and his as he pulled her desperately into his arms and started to kiss her. Oh, those kisses! Hungry, frantically sensual, trembling, moist, passionate. They swamped her at once, almost threatening to drown her.

She was hardly able to breathe…and then she didn't want to. Even unshaven and smelling of wine as he was, his kisses were like heaven. She'd never been kissed like that before.

Or since.

If she'd had any idea beforehand that he would feel so good, so right, perhaps she'd have been able to summon the strength to resist, or the mental space to work out how wrong and impossible this was. But she hadn't, and there was simply no room in her whirling brain for anything but sensation, wonder and growing physical arousal.

He wasn't a very gentle or patient lover that night. The whole thing plunged along like a runaway horse, swift and unstoppable. Hands everywhere. Sobs of hunger and desperation. Torn fabric. If there was any chance to pause for thought or words or breath then one of them might have been able to call a halt.

She didn't care that he wasn't gentle, though, and he didn't hurt her. He just closed his eyes and disappeared into the same turbulent world of the senses that she was experiencing.

And when it was over, and she was still gasping and pulsing with its aftermath, she didn't pause either. She pulled away from him, too stunned and overwhelmed to touch his heated skin any longer.

She scrambled to her feet and gabbled, 'I'm going to have a shower.'

Which she did in the small *en suite* bathroom that opened off her bedroom, standing under the hot needles of water for a good ten minutes as if this might have the power to wash the clock backwards and undo what she and Malcolm had just done.

How is he going to feel in the morning? she thought over and over again. Just how much is he going to hate himself? And me? How much wine did he have? Enough that he won't remember at all? Oh, please, let it turn out that he doesn't remember! *I* can live with it, but can he? I must do whatever is necessary so that this doesn't add to everything he already feels about Bronwyn and Gabrielle.

Six years later, and that huge need to protect him, to spare him, hadn't gone away. What it meant now was very simple.

There are only two ways he must think of me—as a nurse, and as Charlotte's mother. And that's how I must think of him, too—the head of the department I'm working in, and the father of my little girl's best friend.

CHAPTER THREE

MALCOLM stopped Lucy in the A and E entrance the next afternoon, just as she was leaving.

The promised change had come earlier than expected the day before, and the sense of tense anticipation had subsided. Casualties from the bushfires had been fewer than feared, and the hospital had treated only two cases of serious burns and one of smoke inhalation. Still, there was a lot of fuel around for fires, and the bushfire season was by no means over.

'Thank goodness!' Malcolm said. 'The boss wouldn't have been too happy if I'd had to report I'd just missed you.'

'The boss?' Lucy frowned. Was this some administrative problem delivered from on high, concerning her employment conditions or something?

'Yes.' He grinned. 'The female who makes my life miserable on a daily basis, who dictates everything from what we have for breakfast to the city we live in—Miss Gabrielle Lambert.'

'Oh, of course.' She smiled back. 'I should have realised.'

'That I'm under Ellie's thumb?' he suggested.

'That you're not under the thumb of anyone here.'

'Don't let Kerry Anderson hear you say that. She'll rise to the challenge and prove you wrong.'

'Is Ellie demanding another play-date, then?' Lucy asked, making a deliberate decision to return to the issue at hand. She was wary of the fact that they could bat mildly clever lines back and forth like this so easily. It wasn't what she wanted.

'Worse than that, I'm afraid,' he answered. 'She's salvaged that half-hearted commitment we made on Friday to share a meal, dusted it off and polished it up into a pristine, shining promise.'

'Oh, I was afraid of that…'

'So, for the sake of my life expectancy, I said I'd ask you if you and Charlotte were available tomorrow evening. Charlotte can come home with Ellie and Jenny after school, you'll have a couple of hours to yourself and you can join us at my place at about six-thirty when, with any luck, I'll have been home just about long enough to pretend that I cooked the meal myself.'

Of course, Lucy had to laugh at that and, of course, she had to accept, although he helpfully offered some suggested ways of backing out. 'For example, if you were washing the cat, or taking your hair to the vet, or something.'

'Do you want me to be?' she returned, after another laugh. He hadn't been this funny six years ago. How could he have been? 'If so, I can arrange it, I guess,' she went on. 'Haven't actually *got* a cat, but the RSPCA might oblige.'

'No, I don't want you to be,' he said. 'We may as well let our daughters dictate the pace. There are worse things than being roped into a friendship between two little girls.'

'There are.'

'Then it's agreed. Good. Is Charlotte fussy about her food?'

'Nothing with mushrooms, please. Other than that, just keep it simple.'

'Hamburgers?'

'Perfect!'

They were already sizzling in a pan on his stove when she arrived the next evening.

Malcolm only lived about three kilometres from her own house, in an area that was somewhat more expensive and exclusive but not intimidatingly so. It wasn't where he and Bronwyn had been living six years ago, of course.

His house was set high on a steep block of land, backing onto the wild lower slopes of Black Mountain. Lucy found that she actually had to go under one cantilevered wing of the house, through a lush garden of shade-loving ferns, to reach his front door.

'Isn't it an exciting house, Mummy?' Charlotte whispered after an exuberant hug. 'The garden is just like a jungle. Come and look out this window, then come and see Ellie's room.'

Lucy threw an apologetic glance at Malcolm. 'You have a new hostess, apparently. Charlotte, love, Ellie's dad might not want you showing me his house as if it belongs to you.'

'Actually, it's fine.' He laughed. 'Because I got home a little early today and foolishly attempted a rather ambitious salad. You'll distract me if we get talking, and I'll forget to put something vital in the dressing.'

Somehow, Lucy didn't quite believe that. She'd already witnessed several examples at work over the past three days of Malcolm Lambert's ability to do six things at once. She couldn't imagine that merely two—cooking and talking—would throw him off stride. Perhaps it was an excuse. He'd prefer it if she spent the time until dinner with Ellie and Charlotte, rather than with him.

Did he feel more awkward about this whole situation than he showed, then? At work, she wouldn't have guessed that. But at work, of course, there was far too much else going on.

'Do show me, then, Char,' she said brightly to her daughter, and was taken on a very talkative and very detailed ten-minute tour, picking up Ellie on the way.

'This is Ellie's asthma inhaler, Mummy.'

'But I haven't needed it for ages.'

'And this is her favourite doll. Isn't she gorgeous?'

'Her name is Rosalinda Loveheart Splendourfiore. Daddy and I thought of that together.'

'And *she* is splendour-fiorious, isn't she, Mummy? Even nicer than my Debbie. Except I'm not going to call her just Debbie any more. Ellie is going to help me think of a better name.'

Lucy was fascinated…and oddly churned up…by the relationship that was strengthening and developing daily between the two girls. Physically, Ellie seemed so small and frail compared to farm-bred Charlotte, and Lucy knew that Malcolm's concerns in the past about his daughter's health would have been well founded. Charlotte was the more talkative, too.

Despite this apparent dominance, however, Ellie was by no means the humble follower. She had a wonderfully well-developed imagination—witness the elaborate name and even more elaborate life history of the fair Rosalinda—and Charlotte was both spellbound and stimulated by this.

Lucy could fully understand that Debbie, named after one of the sheepdogs on Granny's and Grandad's farm, was simply not going to make the grade from now on. She only hoped she could help Charlotte come up with something suitably 'splendour-fiorious' in its place.

When their tour was finished, having encompassed most of Ellie's possessions but very little of the house itself, Malcolm announced that dinner was ready and the girls set the table. This left Malcolm and Lucy briefly alone together in the bright, modern kitchen.

She seized the opportunity to ask him, 'Has there been any friction between them today?'

'Not since I've been home,' he answered. 'And Jenny didn't mention anything.Why? Has Charlotte been upset?'

'No, not at all. I was just thinking how beautifully they seem to mesh together and wondered if there *was* friction that I hadn't happened to hear about.'

'Not that I know of.'

'It seems unnatural!'

'Don't borrow trouble,' he drawled, and his grey eyes twinkled. 'I'm sure they'll *have* to argue at some point, if the friendship lasts.'

As if to confirm this theory, they both heard raised voices coming from the dining room just a moment later. 'No, *I* was going to do the cutlery!'

'No, *I* was!'

'But you did the plates.'

'Funny, from here I can't even tell whose voice belongs to who,' Malcolm observed.

Lucy nodded quickly. 'All little girls sound the same.'

'Do you think so?'

'When they're fighting at least.'

'I expect you're right,' he conceded.

The girls weren't fighting any more by the time the two adults brought in the food. Lucy noticed that Charlotte looked a little sulky, so perhaps the decision on the cutlery hadn't gone her way. She soon recovered her spirits, however, and they shared a delightful meal.

The girls munched on hamburger patties sandwiched

in buns with tomato sauce and lettuce, while Malcolm and Lucy had their patties with salads. Malcolm's ambitious experiment was a delicious success, and they each drank a glass of wine. Red wine, which only assumed significance later.

Of necessity, the conversation was pitched mostly at five-year-old level, but the girls finished eating first and received permission to leave the table and go and play so that Malcolm and Lucy were alone once more.

Can I really do this? Lucy found herself wondering. I don't think I can. It's bound to be difficult, under the best of circumstances, if a single father and a single mother find that their children are best friends. I expect it happens reasonably often these days when there are so many single-parent families around. Children end up as matchmakers for their parents. But not this time. Not when we have to work together, and when we both only want to forget about what happened that awful night after Bronwyn's death.

'Shall I put on some music?' Malcolm asked. 'Or the news?'

Lucy realised she had been silent for too long. 'Whichever you want,' she answered quickly.

'Music, I think,' he decided. 'Ellie and Charlotte are playing in the living room, and I don't always think the news makes suitable viewing for children.'

He went to the compact disc player in the next room, leaving Lucy with time to start plotting.

Could she possibly manage to break up Charlotte's friendship with Ellie? How? Change schools? That would be the only way, and there were half a dozen arguments against it. Charlotte had only just started there. She was happy. It was close by. It had a very sensible approach to dealing with gifted children...

Lucy heard the sound of her daughter's laughter—or maybe it was Ellie's—once more, just before Malcolm's music began to swell.

No, I won't do it. I *couldn't*! she realised, and it had nothing to do with the issue of schools. Quite simply, she knew she wouldn't be able to bring herself to deliberately break up such a successful and happy friendship, and that was the only thing that counted. The baggage that came with this friendship she would just have to live with, no matter what it cost.

'I'll put on the jug for tea or coffee, shall I?' she suggested to Malcolm ten minutes later, when they'd finished eating.

He nodded, 'Yes, do.'

So they stayed at the table and drank their hot drinks while the two girls played, and it was all quite dangerously, seductively pleasant.

They even washed up together. It took three rounds of polite protests on the subject before he agreed to let her help, and as soon as they'd started she wished she'd let him win on the issue, because they'd done this together too many times before.

She didn't need the reminder of those sad, weary evenings six years ago when they'd rinsed and stacked plates, wiped down bench tops and scoured saucepans in each other's company. Often silent, sometimes talking, never ill at ease with each other.

She could still remember some of their conversations.

'Today, for the first time, I really felt she'd accepted it,' Malcolm had said one evening.

'Did she say something?'

'Not overtly. But she was holding my hand, and...'

'Don't talk about it, Malcolm, if you don't want to.'

'But I do. I *do*! I need to! Oh, damn!'

There had been a splintering, high-pitched sound at this point, because he'd dropped a glass. She'd cleared it up for him at once, and he'd barely even noticed. He'd still been aimlessly wiping an already spotless sink, staring at it without even seeing it as he'd tried to articulate what he'd felt, and what he and Bronny had said to each other.

Not for the first time, Lucy had sensed that it hadn't been an easy, effortless marriage by this time. They'd been together, she'd known, for twelve years, and married for nine. He'd only been eighteen when they'd first met, while Bronwyn had been a year older. Had their difficulties been purely sourced in Bronwyn's illness, or would they have cropped up anyway?

Perhaps no one would ever know. Her illness had been an unavoidable presence in their marriage, and to imagine it away and conjecture about their lives and their relationship without it had been impossible.

Even Lucy's own life had been irrevocably changed because of it. If Bronwyn hadn't been dying, Lucy and Malcolm would never have met, would never have made love, would never have—

'Finished,' Malcolm said, pulling her back across six years to the present. 'A quarter to eight already.'

'Past Charlotte's bedtime,' Lucy answered. 'I'd better get home. She still finds school very tiring.'

'So does Ellie. I have to make sure she— But hang on, we had this conversation the other day, didn't we?' he interrupted himself, then grinned wryly. 'Sorry.'

'It's all right.' She laughed. 'Everyone does it. I'm afraid I lead rather a routine life these days. Subjects for conversation are finite.'

She looked up at him, still with an easy smile on her face, and found that he was looking at her.

'I suppose so,' he said. 'But do you really think that you and I have covered them all already?'

It had been lightly said. Or had meant to be. But Lucy knew that Malcolm was thinking of past evenings spent together now, too, and had belatedly realised that his words had been a little too resonant, a little too significant.

Suddenly their presense together in this airy kitchen wasn't safe any more. Not safe for Lucy, anyway, with her vivid memories. Malcolm's own memories had to be fuzzier, with the wine factored into it, but at the moment that didn't seem to indicate that they were any the less powerful.

'I— Not that I want to revisit— Damn!' he finished expressively.

'It's all right,' she assured him, speaking too fast. 'I'll tell Charlotte it's time for us to go. Thanks, Malcolm. The girls have enjoyed themselves famously, of course, and the meal was delicious. I'll reciprocate, obviously.'

'Don't feel that you have to.'

'Believe me, I have to!' She chuckled, forcing it a little. 'Do you really think Charlotte would let me get away with *not*?'

'This is all for the sake of the girls, isn't it?' he said quietly.

He'd hung up the last teatowel and put away the last glass, and now he was standing in the doorway next to the cupboard where the glassware was kept, leaning his forearm on the frame. He wasn't quite blocking Lucy's path as the doorway was wide, but she would have had to brush right past him to get to the living room, and at that moment she just wasn't prepared to do it.

Neither was she prepared to go the long way around,

through the kitchen's other door behind her. It would have looked like much too significant an avoidance.

'Yes, it *is* for the sake of the girls,' she answered him. 'Isn't that the best reason in the world?'

'It is,' he agreed. 'But does it seem like such a sacrifice to you?'

'Yes. It does.'

'You weren't to blame for what happened six years ago, Lucy.' He was still watching her, his eyes raking over her body as if he could see its sudden heat of awareness.

'Nor were you,' she replied. 'That doesn't change the fact that it was wrong.'

'Wrong *then*.'

'Yes.'

'But there's nothing wrong with what we're doing now, is there? Fostering a successful friendship…an *ideal* friendship, I'd go so far as to say…between our two daughters by making it possible for them to get together outside school hours. Don't get tense about it, please. Don't act as if there's something dangerous about it.'

'Dangerous? Of course there isn't! That's— Your word choice is too confrontational, sometimes, Malcolm.'

'You prefer euphemisms?'

'I prefer accuracy! And I'm not tense.' But she couldn't lie to him in such a bold-faced way. '*Trying* not to be,' she amended more honestly. 'Because I agree with you. I want this for Charlotte. I wish we didn't even have to think about anything else.'

'We don't. We won't. That's what I'm trying—very clumsily—to say. I'm asking you to weather this…this inevitable initial awareness, because of the past, until it fades. Which it will.'

'Do you think so?'

'Yes! New memories and new events will overlay it. The link is only one of memory, and it will be broken. Since, otherwise, yes, it's too uncomfortable for both of us. We both want it. To forget that dreadful, sinful mistake. And so we will.'

'OK.' She nodded carefully. For a man, he was unusually courageous in talking about difficult things. 'Your attitude makes— Well, I like your confidence that *wanting* it will be enough. I—I'm not— Perhaps we—'

'We've said enough, haven't we?'

'Yes. I think so.'

'I can hear the girls getting tetchy with each other again. Let's get them to bed.'

He straightened in the doorway, then stood back to let her through so that she had no choice now. She had to pass close to him, and it was every bit as hard as she'd known it would be. Again, easier for him! Alcohol must have blunted the details. He couldn't possibly remember her body as clearly as she remembered his.

Even the way he smelt. It hit her as she brushed past, that potent mixture of soap and salt and wine. Red wine. That was what he'd binged on that night six years ago. She hadn't even thought of it over dinner, but now it came flooding back. Smell was the most evocative of the senses, and right now it seemed to have the power to carry every other sense along with it.

Hearing. The sound of his shuddering groans and incoherent words. Touch. The feel of her hands kneading his shoulders and pressing flat against his chest. Taste…

My God, had she *tasted* him that night? Yes. She had. She'd pressed her lips against his neck, almost biting him. She'd licked the wine from the corners of his mouth. She'd run the tip of her tongue down his neck until she'd reached the springy curls of hair on his chest and had tasted them, too. She'd pressed her mouth hungrily against his shoulder, his jaw, his forehead, mapping each different sensation in her sense memory as if she needed to have it with her for ever.

She was passing him now, but could feel his hand behind her, hovering at the small of her back, not quite touching her there but getting so close that if she'd hesitated for a second in her stride his palm would have rested there as a warm support.

She wanted it, and it would have been so easy. Perhaps the only thing that gave her the strength to resist was that two-edged sword, her memory. She remembered how quickly and easily the flame of passion had been ignited between them six years ago. If their bodies still sang in harmony the way they once had, then a single hand against her back might well be more than enough.

'Time to go, Charlotte,' she told her daughter brightly.

'Oh, Mummy, no, not yet!'

'Past your bedtime already, love, and both of you have school tomorrow.'

'Well, then, Ellie's going to have to come and have dinner at my place, *soon*!' Charlotte threatened, in the sort of truculent tone which Lucy wouldn't normally have let her get away with.

Tonight, all she cared about was getting her daughter home, so she simply threw an apologetic glance at Malcolm, managed a few more polite comments about the evening and a goodnight to Ellie, and bustled her daughter down under the house through the ferny greenery to the car.

Considering that they hadn't touched at all, it was incredible how her skin crawled and her pulses jumped and the heat coiled inside her.

The sound of the ambulance siren keening outside didn't fully impinge on Malcolm's consciousness at first on this Monday morning. Much of the time it wasn't something he needed to know about, and he could continue, as he was doing now, with the administrative work that occupied a significant percentage of his time.

He'd learnt to follow an almost instinctive interpretation of the sounds he heard to decide whether or not he would be needed, and he was rarely wrong about it these days. There would be an urgency in the pace of footsteps, the pitch of voices, the bump and squeak of equipment and trolleys, and he had usually reached the nerve centre of his department before he was summoned.

That wouldn't happen this time, he suspected.

Yes, the siren had been switched off already, and the ambulance wasn't even coming to his entrance. It had gone past, probably on its way to the outpatient building. He returned his attention to the papers on his desk and began to grapple, once more, with a thorny budgetary problem.

Ten minutes later another siren sounded, and this time it was different. He wasn't surprised when he had to abandon the column of figures he was adding on a calculator, and he only just had time to mark where he was up to with a quick blue slash of his ballpoint pen.

'Patient wheelchair-bound, lost control on a ramp at a shopping centre,' Lucy summarised, repeating what the ambulance officers must have told her. 'He's unconscious, but they don't know why. Doesn't look good.'

As Lucy spoke, Dr Heather Woodley was quickly stripping off the man's clothes, looking for any obvious sign of an injury that could have resulted in loss of consciousness. She was a third-year resident in emergency medicine, and she was competent if occasionally a little narrow in her focus, Malcolm considered.

His mind was running on two levels at that moment. He was very aware of both Lucy and Heather. He didn't like the fact that having them both hovering over this patient provided a disturbing juxtaposition. Intense Heather, and tranquil, good-humoured Lucy. And he was thinking as a doctor, too, with a level of experience that made even this sense of crisis familiar and incapable of making him lose his cool.

The unconscious man looked to be about twenty, give or take a couple of years. He was short, and he wore baggy cargo pants and a loose T-shirt which came down almost to his knees and was printed with lettering. The white block capitals on the purple background read, WHAT'S IT TO YOU?'

It was the fashionable, in-your-face dress of a young man, but his body wasn't well proportioned. He was slightly overweight and the outfit probably served as camouflage as well. There was a marked contrast between the strongly developed shoulders, arms and torso, the curved spine and the under-developed leg muscles, and as soon as his clothes were off they knew why.

'Spina bifida,' Heather Woodley said. 'Look, the scarring at his lower spine is quite obvious. He must have had further surgery since the initial closure of the opening there.'

He had a very pleasant and quite handsome face,

though, set off by short mid-brown hair. Malcolm took in fair, slightly freckled skin, thick dark lashes, a high forehead, a strong nose and a sensitive mouth, all looking relaxed.

'The wheelchair ran down the ramp, out of control, and hit a wall,' Lucy was saying. 'He's got grazing on his face and a bruised shoulder. Look.'

'Is he unconscious due to the crash into the wall?' Malcolm asked.

'Presumably,' Dr Woodley said. 'Apparently, no one was really watching until they realised the wheelchair was out of control.'

She was touching him with her gloved hands.

'OK.' Malcolm nodded.

But he had a bad feeling about this one. It didn't seem right, and his mind was moving at lightning speed. Yes, there were some slight bruises and scratches to the young man's face and shoulder, consistent with a hefty scrape and bump against a brick wall, but the rest of the picture didn't fit.

He took a few seconds to step back mentally, and said half under his breath, 'We're jumping in too soon here. What have we missed? Why are we assuming that he's unconscious because of the fall?'

He added aloud, 'He had no ID? Because he looks vaguely familiar to me…'

'Just some cash in his hand, apparently,' Lucy answered. 'He must have popped out for milk or something.'

'Cigarettes,' Malcolm suggested. 'You can tell by the smell of his clothes that he's a smoker. And I'm sure I know him.' He felt that if the young man would only open his eyes, it would click.

'Previous admission? I wonder what for,' Heather

Woodley said. 'Presumably somehow related to his condition?'

She was an attractive woman of about thirty, tall and dark with quite a strong jaw and shoulders, warm brown eyes and a slightly awkward, angular way of moving. When Malcolm reluctantly considered the idea that he really should start thinking about women again, asking someone out, Heather was one of the women who came to mind. He couldn't think about that vexing issue now.

'Let's not jump to conclusions,' he said quite abruptly, and lifted the patient's lids to look at his eyes.

Again, his spine prickled and he had a sense of foreboding and recognition. He definitely knew this patient. Those burning blue eyes, with their appearance, at this moment, consistent with compression of the optic nerve...

Heather had nodded and swallowed and looked a little hurt at the impatience in his tone. A final thought flashed through Malcolm's mind. *I really must ask her out soon, if I'm going to.*

Surely she didn't *care* about his opinion, though, did she? On a personal level? He didn't need that sort of pressure. Could any of that vague, reluctant awareness of her as a single, eligible woman have translated into signals?

The possibility weighed on him, even in the midst of this medical crisis, and it was a huge relief to hear Lucy say, 'He must have some mobility. He's not always in the wheelchair. I've just looked at the soles of his shoes, and there's dried mud in the treads.'

'That's consistent with the position of the scarring,' Heather was saying. 'His neural tube must have been open quite low down. Then I'm guessing he had surgery for spinal cord tethering at some stage.'

Then it clicked, just as Lucy said, 'What's happening to his face?'

'Get me the drill and the adrenaline, *now*,' Malcolm said urgently. 'I've just remembered who he is.'

The activity around the patient went into overdrive. Lucy had gone for the adrenaline, and they could all see now how the man's mouth was swelling and his breathing was becoming more laboured. His throat would be swelling rapidly as well, and his blood pressure would be plummeting. He was in full anaphylactic shock, and Heather said aloud what they all understood.

'He must be allergic to latex!' Her wide dark eyes were still fixed on Malcolm, as Nurse Sandra Corman ran for the drill.

'Severely,' Malcolm said. 'But that's not the only thing threatening his life at the moment.'

He didn't wait to watch as Heather prepared a syringe of adrenaline and injected it in the man's upper arm, into the fatty layer beneath the skin. Instead, he took the drill and positioned it on the patient's skull. If he didn't release the cerebrospinal fluid that was building to acute pressure at the brain stem, causing this unconscious state…

It was a spine-chilling sound, that high-pitched metallic whine, and Heather wasn't the only one to wince and hiss at it. It did the trick, though, and the clear fluid that had been building up inside Sam's skull—yes, his name was definitely Sam, Sam Ackland—began to drain through the two holes Malcolm had made.

Meanwhile, the symptoms of anaphylactic shock had subsided, and Lucy had hunted up a box of plastic gloves to replace the latex ones which had triggered the dramatic reaction. For the moment, the tension could ease a little.

'His name is Sam Ackland,' Malcolm said as he continued to work, setting up a drip so that a rapid infusion of fluids could correct the patient's dangerously lowered blood pressure. 'And he was in here with bronchitis and pneumonia and acute respiratory failure a couple of years ago. He had a dangerous weight problem then, and was very unfit, but he looks like he's in far better shape now.'

'Yes, look at his shoulders,' Heather said.

'That's one of the reasons I didn't recognise him at first,' Malcolm said, nodding. 'Hell, I feel angry with him! He's obviously done really well with the weight and exercise, but he must have been having symptoms of fluid pressure on the brain. He has a shunt, and it looks as if it must have failed for some reason. Why did he ignore the symptoms? He'd have been having some pretty uncomfortable ones—headaches, sleepiness, maybe even vomiting. Possibly other things like swallowing difficulties, neck pain, weakness in the arms. And he's by no means out of the woods yet.'

'You mean permanent impairment to the brain?' Heather Woodley frowned.

'Unfortunately, yes.' Malcolm nodded. 'We'll send him along to Radiology for a CAT scan, and then he'll be admitted to one of the neurosurgeons. Nick Blethyn, probably. Ultimately, he'll need to have that shunt checked out thoroughly, and probably replaced. We won't know for a few days whether he's escaped permanent damage or not. For that matter, we won't know if he's going to survive…'

He heard Lucy give a shocked hiss.

'Does he have family we can contact?' she asked at once, and Malcolm thought that it was typical of the Lucy he'd known six years ago, who'd always been so quick to think of family and how other people felt. In those essentials, she obviously hadn't changed.

'There may be someone who's frantic at the moment because he didn't come home when expected,' she finished.

'Yes, the fact that he wasn't carrying a wallet, only that handful of cash…'

'Two five-dollar notes.'

'Suggests he wasn't planning to be out for very long,' Malcolm agreed.

He couldn't remember the young patient's personal circumstances. Someone would have to dig out a file. Why wasn't Sam wearing a medical alert bracelet? With his level of allergic response to latex, he had no excuse not to. There was a list a mile long of common products with latex in them. Balloons, tennis balls, wheelchair cushions, clothing elastic, chewing gum, carpet backing… It went on.

And studies were starting to show that up to forty per cent of people with spina bifida had some degree of allergy to the substance. Sam was one of the worst affected, and the allergy had probably intensified with earlier exposure during surgery.

Malcolm felt a wash of helplessness. He hated patients like this. *Hated* them, in a way that had nothing to do with his professionalism as a doctor and everything to do with his personal past. He knew why this patient, and this patient's eyes, had stuck in his mind for two years or more. Sam was exactly like Bronny. Full of fight and anger, but fighting all the wrong things.

He had to struggle mightily against the urge to get angry himself and just start yelling at the unconscious man, Do you know you could be dead before we can get a neurosurgeon to deal with that shunt properly? *If* that's the problem! You haven't exactly given us a lot of time to find out. You could have died of anaphylactic shock, too. Why the *hell* didn't you take your symptoms and your condition seriously?

He said all of this and more inside his head, but managed to resist saying it aloud. Not much point, when a man was unconscious.

Sam was wheeled off to Radiology a few minutes later, after a search through the files had given them his full name and address. His parents were preparing to come in at once, deeply alarmed. They'd told receptionist Caroline Tully that Sam wasn't living at home any more. He'd been living in a flat on his own for the past three weeks, and he'd forbidden them to get in touch with him or come over to see him more than once a day.

'I only hope he makes it,' Malcolm muttered as Sam departed. The matter was out of his hands now, and into the lap of fate…and the neurosurgeon. 'I'll be so *angry* with him if he doesn't!'

'Lucy, there's a three-year-old with a fracture just come in with his mother,' Malcolm heard behind him, the words spoken by another nurse. 'Playground accident, apparently. Can you deal with it? He'll probably have to go up to the children's ward before it can be set.'

'Of course,' Lucy answered. 'I'm finished here.'

'And then Mr Warren is supposed to go up to the cardiac ward, but they've just rung to say the bed's not available yet, so can you make him comfortable here for another couple of hours? And after that, you'll have to…'

He didn't hear any more of the continuing list of instructions, just heard Lucy's laugh floating back as she headed out to the waiting area at the front of the department. He suddenly realised that her voice and her laugh had already become two of the sounds he listened for most eagerly here each day, far more than he listened for Heather Woodley's voice, although he'd known and liked Heather now for over a year.

The long column of budget estimates mocked him when he returned to it several minutes later, and the untidy blue mark beside the thirty-fifth number positively jeered. He'd completely forgotten what it meant. Had he marked the last figure he'd added, or the figure he had to add next? For the life of him, he didn't know.

With a frustrated sigh, he pressed the 'clear' button on the calculator and started keying in the figures from the beginning.

CHAPTER FOUR

'ARE you ever going to get married again, Mummy?' Charlotte asked, with her last mouthful of scrambled egg and toast still evident in her mouth.

Lucy was shocked—far too shocked to even think about the offence to good manners inherent in Charlotte speaking with her mouth full. 'I—Why—? Um, what makes you ask that, love?' she managed finally, trying to infuse it with the same calm, upbeat interest with which she greeted knotty questions about Adam and Eve or the meaning of infinity.

'I just wanted to know.'

Of course. Ask a silly question, get an obvious answer.

She tried again. 'I mean, were you thinking that you'd like me to, or *not* like me to, or something?'

Charlotte's use of the word 'again' was nagging at Lucy's conscience as she spoke.

She'd never actually said that she'd been married to Lucy's father. She'd given as little detail as possible, and had couched it in general terms. They'd only spoken about it together a couple of times, and not for quite a while. There was a big difference between what you told a three-year-old, and what a five-year-old wanted to hear.

But even at three, Lucy had *not* wanted to lie to the extent of telling Charlotte that her daddy was dead. Instead, she'd explained how sometimes a mummy and a daddy found out that they couldn't get on well enough together and it was best if they didn't have anything more to do with each other. They decided which person the child would live with. Often the mummy. Sometimes the daddy.

Sometimes the daddy had visits with the child, or had her to stay in the holidays or on weekends. But some mummies and daddies didn't think this was a good idea. They thought it would be confusing and upsetting for the child, and that it was best if the daddy didn't see the child at all.

All of which had seemed to work very nicely, in answer to 'Why haven't I got a daddy?' up on the farm, when Charlotte had been little, with a wonderful male influence in the person of Grandad. Till very recently, Charlotte had had far more curiosity about the natural world around her than about a father she'd never seen, and she'd had little daily contact with other children and their sophisticated ideas and modern family relationships.

Now, suddenly, out of the blue, the difficult questions had started.

'I don't know if I'd like you to or not,' Charlotte said. 'I wouldn't know that, would I, until I'd met the man that you were thinking of having be my new dad? If I liked him, then I'd like a new dad. I've never had a proper one before, and it'd be fun. Ellie's dad is fun. But if I didn't like him, then I'd tell you that, and you'd tell him, 'No, I can't marry you', wouldn't you?'

Charlotte obviously wasn't saying all this off the top of her head. She must have been thinking about it very seriously.

'Well,' Lucy managed, feeling almost dizzy at the hypothetical heights she and Charlotte were ascending to, out of the blue. Charlotte was due at school in twenty minutes, and her school lunch wasn't made and Lucy was still in her slippers. 'I don't think I'd get as far as having him ask me to marry him if you didn't like him. I think if you and he didn't get along well together after you'd met each other a couple of times, I'd tell him...tell him...'

'That you wouldn't marry him, like I said,' Charlotte supplied helpfully.

'Well, no, because people don't usually talk about getting married until they know each other very, very well.'

'Like for a whole term?'

'Usually longer than that.'

'*Two* terms?'

'Sometimes two terms.' Now Lucy felt as if she was being pulled very cheerfully farther and farther down a path that was in completely the opposite direction from where she wanted to go, and she knew she had to take firm control of the conversation. 'You've been talking about this with someone, haven't you? Was it a teacher?'

'Are you cross?'

'No, I'm not cross, gorgeous, but I would like to know.'

'It was Ellie. She talks about it with her dad. Her dad says he thinks he might get married again, but not yet. You see, it wasn't that he and Ellie's mum couldn't get on together. She died when Ellie was a baby. Ellie doesn't remember her. Isn't that sad? I couldn't *bear* it if you died, and I think Ellie's dad is still sad about it.'

'I expect he is,' Lucy agreed carefully. 'People stay sad about things like that for a long time.'

'And he asked Ellie if she'd like him to get married

again, and she said she didn't know, and he said to think about it, so she did, and she decided the same as me.'

'Right. I see. Was...was that recently?'

'Yesterday. At breakfast.'

'Ellie's dad must be more awake in the mornings than I am, then!'

And he was, she remembered. He was one of those people who bounced out of bed in full possession of his faculties, whereas she needed to be jolted into it—as she just had been—or coaxed into it with the long hot shower she hadn't had time for this morning.

Speaking of time...

'Charlotte, we'll have to finish talking about this another time,' she said desperately, 'or we'll both be late.'

'I've finished talking about it, anyway,' Charlotte assured her comfortably. Evidently, Lucy had managed to allay any underlying doubt or anxiety, although that had to be good luck, not good management, as she knew she hadn't handled the subject particularly well.

Was that because the whole conversation had been built on tacit untruths she'd hidden behind for years?

For now, the question had to stay unanswered, and she convinced Charlotte so thoroughly of the disastrousness of being late that they tumbled out of the house together in good time. The breakfast dishes weren't done, but who cared?

In front of the school, Charlotte jumped out of the car at once and rushed off to greet a friend who also came to before-school care. On the short journey to work, the traffic flow and both sets of lights went Lucy's way. The result was that, instead of being late, as she'd feared, she arrived a good ten minutes early. The bright morning sun was just starting to heat up the air that had chilled overnight, and the sulphur-crested

cockatoos were screeching at each other in the tall eu-
calyptus trees that surrounded the hospital.

Knowing that she'd get roped into work the moment
she set foot in the department, Lucy decided to go up
to the neurological ward to see how Sam Ackland was
getting on. It was four days since he had passed through
their department, and yesterday afternoon, at last, they'd
had a good report from the ward.

The shunt, as suspected, had stopping working as it
should. Malcolm's emergency draining of the fluid
which had been pressing on Sam's brain had very probably saved his life, and neurosurgeon Nick Blethyn had
found that the shunt was now too short, following
Sam's recent spurt of growth to his adult height of 154
centimetres.

Dr Blethyn had replaced it with a shunt of the correct
length, and physically Sam had handled the surgery
well. Full precautions had been taken against triggering
another allergic reaction to latex. Vinyl gloves, silk tape
and plastic catheters had been used. Sam had regained
consciousness the previous morning, although it wasn't
yet known how much, if any, permanent brain damage
he'd sustained. So far, the signs were good.

Further tests showed that the fluid was now moving
through the new shunt properly, and it would be
checked again at intervals, with a series of X-rays over
the entire length of the shunt and tubing.

This morning, Sam was well enough to have the upper end of the bed raised, and he could manage a light
and mostly liquid diet. He was also well enough to dis-
dain such a diet and was insisting to a nurse when Lucy
walked in, 'Take it away! Yuck!'

The blonde nurse, Sally, whom Lucy knew by this

time from one or two lunches at the same table in the hospital dining room, was unperturbed by his rudeness.

'You're doing great, Sam,' she said cheerfully. 'I love it when you guys get hungry. Then I know you're really on the mend!'

'So can I have eggs?'

'No!' she taunted him gently. 'Maybe tomorrow. Ask your doctor when he comes round.'

She rolled her eyes at Lucy as she left the room, but she was smiling at the same time. 'We really didn't know what you lot had sent us this one for,' she said, deliberately speaking loudly enough for Sam to hear. 'We weren't convinced he was going to be here long enough to warrant changing the bed linen. But listen to him!'

Sam laughed with some effort, then turned at once to Lucy and wanted to know, 'Who the heck are you?'

'You weren't in a fit state to remember,' she agreed calmly. 'I work in the emergency department, where you got admitted on Monday.'

'Oh, OK.'

'Yeah, we're the ones who had to guess what was wrong with you because you'd decided not to provide us with any little hints, like ID or a medical alert brace-let,' she told him cheerfully.

'Yeah, well, I used to, but I lost it,' Sam growled.

He seemed a little taken aback by her frankness, but she saw no point in letting him hide from the truth. This young man reminded her of some of the lads who passed through the casualty department of Brewarra Base Hospital. Country boys whose prospects seemed to them to be shrinking in a changing world. Angry, because they were scared. Belligerent, because they didn't know how to ask for help. Denying what was wrong, because maybe will-power would be enough to make it go away.

Lucy had decided some time ago that the tender treatment didn't work with these people. They didn't like a spoonful of sugar with their medicine. Instead, if you just kept on giving it to them straight, they eventually responded. It was usually a simple matter of time. They grew up. They worked out what they wanted, and what was possible. You couldn't rush the process.

She asked Sam casually, 'Planning to get it replaced?'

'I'll get to it.'

'Soon, OK? It isn't obvious from the outside that you've got spina bifida, and the association between that and latex allergy is a pretty recent discovery.'

'Like hell it isn't obvious I've got spina bifida!'

'It could be a spinal cord injury, or a degenerative condition,' she pointed out. 'Until we saw the scarring on your back, we weren't sure.'

He shrugged. 'Does it matter?'

'You tell me!' she suggested lightly. 'I expect it would matter to your parents and your friends if you were ever in another situation like Monday, and there were doctors treating you who didn't know your history and so didn't know what to do. It was lucky Dr Lambert happened to have treated you before.'

She didn't say any more, and was a little afraid that she'd said too much already. He might chew on it a little after she'd left, but would he digest it?

Hearing a voice in the doorway, she turned and got caught in the captivating light of Malcolm's grey-eyed gaze. Her body reacted straight away, heating up as if an infrared lamp had suddenly switched on overhead.

They both jumped into an explanation at once.

'I had a minute, so—'

'I got here a bit early, and—'

Then they laughed. 'Same impulse,' he said. 'You should be flattered, Sam.'

'Flattered?' He blinked.

'We only follow up on the really interesting patients,' Malcolm explained, the dry humour evident in the little tucks at the corner of his mouth. 'The rest we consign to the questionable care of the staff on the higher floors, once we've done the dramatic, life-saving bit down below.'

'So what makes me interesting?' Sam growled. His speech was still slow and a little unsteady, but there were no obvious signs of brain damage. He had been extraordinarily lucky.

'We're taking bets,' Malcolm teased, with a grim edge behind the humour. 'How long before you get brought in again, because you've developed Chiari symptoms and you've ignored the fact that you can't breathe or swallow properly, or because you've got slack with self-cath and with check-ups at your doctor's, and you've got infected urine backing up into your kidneys.'

'Are you saying I shouldn't be living on my own?'

'I'm saying that if you live on your own you've got to look after yourself, and I'm sure I'm not the first person to have said it.'

'You got that right!'

'I happen, however, to be the person who'll have to bring you back from the brink long enough to get you to a surgeon or the ICU, like I had to the other day. It was so close, Sam, *so* close! And if you've left it too late next time, and you go over the brink, I'm the one who'll have to tell your parents, and who'll have your death confronting me over and over again every time I wonder if there was more I could have done. You've done so well with weight loss and fitness since I last saw you. Don't let that count for nothing.'

'You're not really taking bets...'

'No. But I'm tempted, mate. Which side do you think I should put my money on?'

Sam didn't answer at first. He'd closed his eyes and his face looked tight. There was a silence. Then he creaked slowly, 'OK. You made your point. My parents did, too. They yelled last night.'

'After they'd finished squeezing you so tight you practically burst, I expect,' Malcolm suggested.

'Yeah,' he admitted. 'After that.'

'Bye, Sam,' Lucy said. 'Get your parents to chase up a new medical alert bracelet, hey?'

Malcolm added in the same tone, 'Yes, give them something to do. Parents tend to need that, though I know it's a nuisance.'

They were both rewarded with a faint, reluctant smile as Lucy stretched forward to give Sam's shoulder a pat. Then somehow it seemed very natural for them to leave the neurological ward together.

'A bit strong for a moment, there, weren't you?' she commented to Malcolm as soon as they were out of earshot along the corridor, although she'd decided herself that the soft approach would be wrong for this patient. She'd been strong, too, but not nearly as strong as Malcolm.

'Probably,' he answered her.

'Didn't you mean to be?'

'It wasn't rehearsed, if that's what you're asking.'

'Then you lost control.'

'No, I simply made a decision on the spot to air my

real opinion, couched in a little rough humour and a little dramatic imagery, which I hoped he might appreciate later on, even if he doesn't now.'

'Risky.'

'I know. Do you think that's wrong?' he challenged. 'Should we only take physical risks with patients, like thumping them so hard to get their heart restarted that we break a rib? Or drilling their skull open, largely on intuition? Can't we take the occasional emotional risk of that kind, too? Sam's trying to live on his own. That's great, but he just won't make it if he doesn't accept what a responsibility it is. What's better? To yell at him and get him angry, but hopefully thinking? Or tell him he's doing a great job when even *he* knows, deep down, that he isn't? Do we want him slinking back to his parents in a couple of months, feeling like the word 'failure' is tattooed on his forehead?'

'Are those the only choices?'

'*Aren't* they?'

'What about time? I'm a huge believer in time.'

'I'm not,' he answered shortly. 'Bronny's death cured me of that. Sometimes there *isn't* time.'

'But hasn't time healed the grief for you at all?' she asked, confused as she connected his words with what Charlotte had reported that morning. Lord help him, did he still ache for Bronny that much?

And if he does, she thought with a pang, what does that mean for me?

'No, no, you've misunderstood,' he answered. 'I'm talking about *before* she died. The sense that time was this precious commodity and it was just *running out*, and we had a lifetime of things still to say to each other, and—' He stopped. 'Why are we talking about this now?'

'Because…because— I'm sorry.'

'Don't apologise. I want to talk about it. With you. Because you were there…' He hesitated, and there was a faint questioning intonation on the last word. 'I suppose,' he added. 'I suppose that's the reason. But not now. Some time when we can do it properly, with no sense of being rushed.' He laughed. 'Which is exactly what I was talking about. It would be really nice to feel that it didn't have to be like Sam, and like Bronny—so rushed.'

They reached the accident and emergency department and separated. After a quick goodbye to Lucy, Malcolm headed straight for his office, feeling as if the day had already been a long one. He'd dropped Ellie off at Jenny's extra early this morning, and got an hour of administrative work under his belt before taking a break and doing some real medicine—following up on patients who'd passed through the department this week and overseeing the more serious cases admitted over the past few hours.

One patient had died in the early hours of the morning before they'd been able to stabilise his condition, and Heather still looked pretty shattered about it. He saw her standing over by the storage shelves that flanked the open area where trolley patients were initially seen, and if she was actually doing something productive, it wasn't very apparent. She seemed to be staring into space, and she was twisting a finger in her hair like a little girl.

'Come into my office for a minute, Heather,' he suggested, detouring in her direction.

She looked up, focused her gaze and nodded. Two tiny spots of colour flooded into her cheeks. She knew exactly why he wanted to see her.

'You're going to tell me it wasn't my fault,' she began eagerly as soon as the door was half-closed behind her. Malcolm rarely allowed himself the luxury of closing the door completely. 'And I *know* that, but it's still horrible. He was a young man! Only thirty-two. A weightlifter and a boxer. An athlete, in other words. Incredibly fit, and with a wife and a young child. *Why*, Malcolm?'

'Hereditary factors, I expect. Diet? Just because he was fit, it doesn't mean he ate well in terms of fat intake, and so forth. To be honest, I also suspect there was long-term steroid use as a factor in this case.'

'The risks of steroids are pretty widely known...'

'It doesn't stop some people, Heather, you know that.'

They talked about the medical issues for some minutes more, then Heather circled back again to her own feelings. Not that he blamed her. She had a very natural need to talk it out, and nothing she said was inappropriate.

'I can't shake it off. I don't *want* to shake it off. Isn't it important just to...*pause* a little in my life?'

'Yes, Heather, yes, if that's how you feel.'

But before he even finished speaking he saw that she was crying, and so he did the natural thing and took her in his arms. She went willingly, and buried her face in his shoulder. He didn't like the feeling. She was like a persistent cat who was determined on a particular lap for its evening snooze. It almost felt as if she was *burrowing*.

'Oh, Malcolm,' she whispered, her breath coming in jerks. 'Oh, Malcolm, is it always this hard?'

A hell of a lot harder! he wanted to tell her. He knew what he was supposed to do, and every bit of sense and logic and practicality in him told him to do it. Kiss her on the forehead, at the very least! Then ask her out. Dinner tonight, after work, 'to talk it out'.

So easy. So obvious. And clearly what she wanted. They were both single. She was attractive. They had a lot in common.

The first words began to form in his mouth and he found himself looking down at the top of her head as if it were a target, planning the spot where he'd plant the kiss. There, maybe, where her parting was.

Then the sounds of the busy department outside began to impinge. He didn't even have time to disentangle the different strands. Voices. A cupboard opening. The plastic sigh of the swing doors. A laugh that he recognised.

And he knew he couldn't do it, that he'd never be able to do it. It wasn't a question of time, of getting to the end of some metaphorical road named The Grieving Period. He'd reached the end of that road some time ago. The basic fact remained. He just wasn't attracted to Heather Woodley, and he couldn't imagine that anything would ever alter that.

Gingerly, he released her, gave her a last pat on the shoulder and said, 'Better now? Go and mop your face, then try and get back to work. It helps.'

'Thanks,' she answered. 'You've been so good.'

No, I haven't. I've only given you a fraction of what you wanted, he thought. I'd apologise for that, only it would only make things more awkward...

He said aloud, instead, in a bluff, breezy sort of tone, 'All part of the job.'

Then, very deliberately, he turned away so he wouldn't see the disappointment in her face.

*   *   *

The first Friday in March, the end of Lucy's third week in her new job, was humming along much like any other—until lunchtime, that was.

'I had to come in because I broke my crutch,' the patient said. 'Wouldn't have had to come in if I hadn't have broken my crutch.'

'It's lucky you *did* come in,' Lucy said.

Lucy didn't know quite what tone to take with this woman, and was a little on edge. There were some glaring signs that she didn't like in the least, and she knew that Wendy Boyle, who was on triage today, had felt the same. It wasn't the dyed brown hair, growing out at the roots to reveal two inches of grey, or the pitted, leathery skin. It wasn't even the layers of unkempt clothing, rank with the smell of stale cigarette smoke, which suggested that this woman lived a marginal existence and was possibly homeless.

No, it was more the look in her flecked golden eyes. Intelligent, but fearful and restless.

Alphonsine de Crespigny was the name the woman had given, although she wasn't able to produce a Medicare card to prove it. The name seemed unlikely. She was obviously mentally ill. The question was, could she be a danger to herself or to others? If so, she needed to be admitted to the acute psychiatric ward, but Lucy suspected that she wouldn't take the idea well.

It wasn't encouraging that the only problem Alphonsine perceived in her own condition was her broken crutch, battered old thing that it was, and Lucy wondered about her need for crutches in the first place. It looked to be purely to take the weight off painful legs, particularly the left.

The wounds on her legs didn't fit an obvious pattern that would have suggested their cause. Possibly, they were a combination of more than one injury, as well as ongoing neglect. Wendy Boyle had peeled away a few of the makeshift strips of bandage on the right leg, taken one look at what lay beneath and had sent Alphonsine straight back here to the open area of the unit where Lucy had been working all this week.

On a busy day, this patient might have gone into a cubicle and had to wait her turn, but on this Friday afternoon, just on lunchtime, things were quiet in this section of the department, and it was the cubicles which were overloaded with a succession of minor problems.

Alphonsine had refused to removed the bandages on the right leg completely, and hadn't let Wendy touch the left leg at all. As she sat on the trolley on a fresh white sheet, she was busily trying to adjust them and get them back into place, hissing and cursing unintelligibly as they stuck to the oozing, encrusted wounds.

'How did you hurt your legs?' Lucy asked.

'I didn't.'

'Then why are you wearing the bandages?'

'They're not bandages. They're leggings. To keep my legs warm.'

'But it's summer, Mrs de Crespigny.'

'I've got bad circulation, haven't I? And I'm not Mrs de Crespigny. I'm La Comtesse.' The way she said it stressed that it was a noble title.

'Well, it's warm in here, so I'll have to take them off because I need to see—'

'I just need a new crutch.'

And so it went on for several minutes, back and forth. Lucy managed to get the bandages off the right leg, and was horrified at the full extent of the infected wounds she saw. It was impossible to guess at their origin, or how long they'd been there. Clearly, they were getting worse. They would have to be debrided and thoroughly cleaned, and a course of broad-spectrum antibiotics started.

And then Lucy discovered that the right leg was the minor problem. When she finally persuaded this odd woman to let her look at the left, she saw at once that it was grey and pale below the knee. Painful, too. This was the real reason for the crutches, which La Comtesse refused to acknowledge. The smell of cigarette smoke now provided a telling clue. The woman had peripheral vascular disease, and a clot had formed in her lower leg, giving it that tell-tale grey and lifeless appearance.

Lucy felt sick. She'd need a doctor to confirm the diagnosis, but she really wasn't in any doubt. La Comtesse had gangrene, and was going to have to lose her leg below the knee. Breaking such news to a mentally ill patient and getting her prepped for immediate surgery wasn't going to be easy. Her stomach rumbled. It was a quarter past one and she was overdue for lunch. That didn't matter at the moment. She was due to go for her break when Kerry Anderson got back, but Kerry was late for some reason.

She heard Wendy on the phone out in the waiting area, and one of the interns, Jeff Curtis, in a side office complaining about something to Brian Smith. There were several more staff closeted with patients in the cubicles, but there was no one actually in sight at the moment. It was one of those unnatural hiatuses which would soon come to an end, but for the moment it was disconcerting.

'What's your problem?' Alphonsine demanded suddenly. She must have seen the horror in Lucy's eyes. 'What is your problem, *mademoiselle*? You're not thinking you're going to admit me, are you? I'm not getting admitted! That Ward 16, I know that place…'

She swore and lunged up from the trolley where Lucy had got her to lie. Equipment went flying. She yelped about the pain in her left leg. Lucy had begun to try to debride the more superficial and less severely infected wounds on the right leg, buying time as she tried to assess the best way to talk to this patient about her more urgent problem. Should she get a doctor immediately? Heather Woodley? Or Brian Smith? Malcolm? Or should she attempt to build a better rapport first?

With Alphonsine's sudden, violent movement, these questions became irrelevant, and suddenly it wasn't the patient's welfare that consumed Lucy's mind but her own. Alphonsine de Crespigny—what an unlikely, ridiculous name, like one of little Ellie Lambert's dolls—had pushed Lucy back onto the trolley with an almost unnatural show of strength and was pinning her there with a little black gun pressed into her cheek.

Was it real? Lucy had no idea. It *felt* real. Cold and heavy and solid. Was it loaded? It wasn't a situation in which you took chances. Her breathing was coming in rapid, shallow pants, and all she could think of was Charlotte…precious Charlotte, innocently busy at school and mercifully knowing nothing of this.

Or nothing *yet*.

I will not die! I can't take the risk that the gun's a toy, or not loaded, and I *cannot* let her shoot me!

So she simply lay there, trying not to shake, trying not to say or do or even *think* anything that could possibly impel this mad woman to pull the trigger on her little toy. She was treating it like a toy, sliding its cold snub nose across Lucy's cheek, making a clicking sound with it. Lucy was sure now that it was real. And did that clicking sound come from the trigger?

This is ridiculous! she thought. People were wrong when they said, 'I didn't think it would ever happen to *me*!' That's not how this feels. But how did my life go from being so safe and normal one minute to being so fragile and under threat the next? That's how it feels. Sheer astonishment that it could be so sudden. It was just an ordinary day! There ought to have been a *signal*! Oh, as if that matters now…

I *cannot* let her shoot me!

CHAPTER FIVE

COMING back from his lunch-break, such as it was, Malcolm was aware, as Lucy had been, of the unusual quiet in his department.

He did a quick head count in the waiting area on his way through. A dozen people, but at least half of them were the friends and relatives of patients, not the patients themselves. He glanced into a couple of the open cubicles and saw Heather Woodley suturing a gashed hand and Anna Seaman questioning an elderly man about his symptoms. A junior nurse, Lisa Fellowes, was assisting Heather.

Jean and Alison, today's front desk staff, were on the phone. There were a couple more closed doors with the sound of voices behind them. Finally, as he neared his office, he looked along to the trolleys at the far end, which had been completely empty fifteen minutes ago when he'd gone off for a sandwich.

He froze. The trolley end wasn't empty now. There was a woman in a ragged grey coat there, leaning over one of the trolleys, pressing something black into the face of someone in a neat-fitting, pale blue uniform. He heard a voice, thready rather than musical as it usually was, but he still recognised it as Lucy's.

He couldn't hear what she was saying, but he could tell even from this distance that she was scared. The equipment that surrounded her seemed to gleam with menace suddenly, and that little black thing—great goodness, could it be a gun?

He took about five seconds more to assess the situation. Was he really seeing all this? Hell, *yes*…

Silently, he moved closer, prepared to duck into his office if it looked like the woman might see him. Somehow he sensed that the more dangerous trigger wasn't the one on the gun but the one in the woman's own psyche. If she felt threatened and that sent her over the edge…

He began to sweat and to calculate at the same time.

The one positive factor in this situation was that she had her back to him at the moment, because she'd circled around the head end of the trolley to position herself better so that she could look into Lucy's face.

All I need to do is get the gun away, he began to think feverishly. If I can do that before she sees me coming, then I can yell blue murder and I'll have help in keeping her subdued. But I've got to get the gun away *first*… If Lucy sees me coming…she might see me because she's in a better position to see than Grey Coat is…she might be able to distract her and mask any sounds I make.

He had to will his body not to shake as he moved along the corridor, had to remind himself of the old saying about more haste and less speed, but he made steady progress. It felt as if this was taking for ever, but when he caught sight of the wall clock a little further along, he realised that his sense of time passing was out of kilter. It was only a minute…less…since he'd first seen that shocking sight of Lucy and the woman and the gun.

Hardly daring to breathe, he continued his painfully controlled creep closer, and could hear the woman muttering. No, singing. In French. She had the sort of lusty voice that would have done justice to bawdy songs in an old vaudeville show. It was surprisingly tuneful and her French accent was, to his ears, flawless. Lucy must have thought so, too.

'Where did you learn to speak French, Comtesse Alphonsine?'

'Mais, je suis française, ma chère!' She delivered an impeccably correct series of French oaths.

'What was the name of the song you were singing just now?'

'*"Ça ira.*' They used to sing it in the Revolution. This is my revolution, you see.'

'Yes, I see. So you're singing a revolutionary song? I like the tune.'

Had she seen him? Malcolm wondered. She was doing all the right things. Distracting Grey Coat, engaging her, not threatening her, getting her to talk about something positive and safe. He was very close to both of them now, belatedly thinking back to Heather and Brian and Anna and the others.

How close were they to being finished with those patients? If they came out of those cubicles at the wrong moment and made a noise, and Grey Coat turned… Should he have taken the time to involve them? Should he have called hospital security, or the police, or something? Too late now.

And which was the greater risk in the two choices he had next? Lunge now, when he wasn't quite close enough and Grey Coat might have time to pull the trigger? Or wait another critical few seconds until he was closer and risk having her hear him? She was reciting poetry now, still in that flawless, resonant and beautiful French.

Not yet. Not yet. Not yet.

Each step was a silent, rhythmic protest against action. He could hardly believe it when his right hand closed over the gun at last, while at the same time he wrenched the woman's other arm back and up behind her.

She stiffened and screamed, struggled for a moment, then seemed to give up and began sobbing in his arms.

'Brian!' he yelled, turning his head away from the woman's stale, smoky smell. 'I need you here, *now*!'

'Oh, Malcolm, Malcolm...'

On the trolley, Lucy began to shudder convulsively, and if he hadn't been holding a hysterical, mentally ill woman with infected wounds and a grey, gangrenous leg and a gun that was very definitely real, he'd have bent over and pulled her up into his arms and kissed her warm, living flesh a hundred times. The thought of the danger she'd been in was now making every hair on his head prickle as his scalp tightened to the point of pain.

This is why I couldn't ask Heather Woodley out, he suddenly realised. Because if I'm going to ask anyone out, if I'm going to summon up that courage, put my toe in the water of that particular very frightening pool, then it's going to be Lucy.

It was a realisation that had his stomach churning and his heart singing at the same time, and he felt so tangled up inside with fear and hope and pleasure and doubt that he couldn't even look at her.

Everything happened very quickly after that. Jeff Curtis took over the care of the grey-coated woman and managed to get her subdued and onto a trolley. An ambulance siren sounded in the background before Malcolm had said a word to Lucy in response to her feverish use of his name. Brian was crouching beside her, asking if she was OK, and another emergency patient was being brought in, a pale, sweaty man in his fifties in the severe pain of a major heart attack. Malcolm gave him the appropriate drugs and set him up on a heart monitor, his brain still whirling. He heard another ambulance siren approaching from the street outside.

A few minutes later, the grey-coated woman with the gangrenous leg was taken away to be prepped for surgery after orthopaedic surgeon Michael Farrell had confirmed that amputation of the left leg below the knee was the only life-saving option. The patient had given a hazy and grudging consent, although she still insisted that her name was Alphonsine.

Brian took Lucy into one of the cubicles and gave her a glass of brandy and a cup of sweetened tea, then ordered Lisa to sit with her. Kerry was back now, and took over Lucy's tasks. She'd been buttonholed by someone from Administration in the cafeteria. Something to do with a report she'd submitted last week, she said. The remaining staff had returned from lunch as well. Brian went off to deal with the latest emergency admission.

In the space of ten minutes, they'd gone from being abnormally quiet to having a major backlog, but it couldn't be helped. As soon as he'd satisfied himself that the cardiac patient was adequately stabilised, Malcolm said to Heather, 'Can you keep an eye on him, and find out when we can get him up to the ward?'

'They may not have a bed,' she offered.

He knew that, of course. The whole hospital was frequently short on beds at the moment, and would continue to be until a planned extension was completed. There was the issue of budget cuts as well. The fact hardly needed to be mentioned every time. You simply had to negotiate, argue, compromise…and meanwhile make the patients as comfortable as possible.

He almost snapped at Heather, then reminded himself that she must be as tense as he was. Wendy had called the police, and the gun was still sitting on the equipment trolley where Malcolm had very carefully placed it, No one wanted to touch it. Kerry had wheeled the trolley into Malcolm's office and shut the door.

This wasn't a big American city. This was safe, tame Canberra. Half the staff in the department had never seen a gun before, let alone in the hospital. Malcolm himself had only encountered one once, still clutched, no longer loaded, in the hand of the patient who'd accidentally shot himself in the foot while rabbit-hunting. A totally different situation, in other words.

'Lucy!'

At last, after what seemed like hours but wasn't anything like that long, he was able to see her. He instinctively closed the cubicle door behind him to shut out the craziness of the department. Everyone was jittery, and everyone was trying to hide it from the non-urgent patients still waiting their turn to be seen.

Those who hadn't been present during the drama had to be told the story, in quick private murmurs. Heather's voice sounded high and strident, until the door clicked shut and muffled the sound.

'How are you?' he said to Lucy. Hell, he sounded completely useless!

'I'm fine.'

'No, you're not.'

'I'm *alive*, Malcolm. I'm not hurt,' she replied shakily. 'That's all that matters. I just kept thinking that if I died today, how badly would it damage Charlotte? I was so scared, so scared! And now this brandy's going to my head because I haven't had lunch, and I just keep thinking that *I'm alive*! Has she gone to surgery?'

'The woman? Alphonsine?'

'La Comtesse Alphonsine de Crespigny. It can't be her real name, surely, but her French was certainly perfect.'

'Yes, I heard the poetry. She's on her way to surgery, and they're going to remove the lower leg. The other leg will need some treatment, too, and James Nairn from the psychiatric unit will be involved as soon as she's out of Recovery, to try and stabilise her mental condition. It may be schizophrenia, or a form of very severe manic depression. She's clearly a well-educated woman. If her illness can be controlled by medication, then the leg problem may be a blessing in disguise.'

'You mean she might have a normal life she can go back to?'

'It's possible.' He nodded. 'Meanwhile, the police are going to try and track down her next of kin, and they'll need you to decide if you'll press charges.'

Lucy buried her face in her hands. 'That's the last thing I want to do!'

'Don't make a decision now.'

'I *am* making a decision! I won't press charges. She's mentally ill. There'd be no point. And it would mean Charlotte would have to know, and my parents, wouldn't it?'

'I expect so.'

'They don't need that.'

'But what do you need, Lucy?'

'Something to eat, and to get back to work…'

'Post-traumatic stress counselling is practically compulsory. I expect they'll want us both to have some sessions.'

'That, then,' she agreed, as if it didn't matter one way or the other. 'And then time… We were talking about this last week…time to gradually put it behind me.'

'Don't bottle it up.'

'I'm not planning to.' She smiled. 'I'm planning to vent it in a very long walk on the beach this weekend after Charlotte has gone to bed.'

'You're going down to see your parents?'

'Yes, I've been planning it for weeks, and now I can't wait!'

She was thinking of it already—the glorious stretches of open, uncrowded beaches, the rolling blue-green waves. The option, if she needed it—and she suspected she would—to run and shout and scream, with the sound safely masked by the waves. She was still thinking about it, pinning herself to it, actually, when Malcolm spoke again, and his words dragged her back from her visions of the ocean and took her by surprise.

'I'm really glad for your sake that you're going down to your parents',' he said slowly, 'but I have to admit to some selfish disappointment as well. I was going to ask if you were free to go out on Saturday evening.'

'Go out? With you?' she said stupidly. *No, with Leonardo di Caprio*, she mocked herself inwardly.

Malcolm was kinder. 'Yes, with me.' His tone was patient. 'But if it's a horrible idea…'

'Of course it isn't,' she said quickly, with automatic politeness. After all, Malcolm Lambert had just saved her life.

'No!' he exclaimed almost angrily. 'Look at me, Lucy!'

She raised her eyes to meet his watchful gaze. 'Yes?'

'I'm not just saying that,' he said urgently. 'You know what happened between us before, and why it was so impossible and wrong. Six years have gone by. I've come to terms with what we did. I've laid my guilt to rest. That didn't happen overnight, and it wasn't easy.'

'Oh, Malcolm, I'm sure it wasn't!'

'But I've done it. And now, seeing you again...I'd like to spend an evening together and talk a bit. There's no one left in my day-to-day life any more from that time. For you, though, I realise that it might be totally different. So I'll say it again. If it's a horrible idea, then you must say so, and we'll never speak about it again. Or if you simply need some time to think...'

'Perhaps I do,' she acknowledged.

The small room was thick with their awareness of each other. That male body, sitting just feet away. She'd held that body against her. She'd squeezed him, cradled him, kissed him, eased him inside her. If they went out together, would it happen again? Did he want it to?

She didn't want it. The idea almost frightened her. Another desperate joining, with no context of love and commitment surrounding it? No! Even thinking about it felt dangerous.

And yet that wasn't the only way in which she'd known him. They'd been...not friends, exactly. More like allies, or partners. Partners in their service to Bronwyn, and partners in the desperate tenderness they'd felt for motherless baby Gabrielle...tiny Gabrielle, who was now Ellie, Charlotte's friend.

Lucy understood, for the first time, that he was the only such partner she'd ever had in her life, and that there had been a wonderful balance and equality between them, innocent, until that final night, of anything dishonest or sinful.

And she understood something else. That she still loved him. Loved the father of her precious only child in a way she'd doubted she'd ever be able to love a man again.

Yes, she loved Charlotte's father as much as she had six years ago, when she'd spared him from even knowing about the devastating fact of Charlotte's conception. In that way, she was still protecting him, deliberately letting him believe that it was her short-lived relationship with Brett back home in Brewarra which had produced her child.

For the first time, she wondered whether Malcolm would thank her for keeping her secret as she had. She'd done it out of love, but might he see it differently, now that they were a part of each other's lives once more?

'You're right, Malcolm,' she went on, after a pause. 'I do need to think about it. Thank you for understanding that before I did.'

'You're hardly in a fit state to think about anything right now,' he pointed out, and they smiled tentatively at each other.

He was about to touch her. She could sense it, although he hadn't moved from his position, standing near the narrow examining table on which she sat. Her skin already crawled with need. But then there was a knock at the door and Jean Jarrett, from the front desk, poked her head around the door.

'The police are here, Malcolm,' she said. 'They want to interview both of you, and have a look at the gun.'

'Me first, if that's all right with them,' he answered. 'Lucy badly needs to get something to eat. Would you like one of us to bring it for you, Lucy?'

A mask had descended over his face now, not hostile or distant, but he was definitely back in his role as the head of the department. It made her realise just how easily and comfortably and honestly they could communicate on a personal level.

'No, I'm fine,' she told him, with the same new professional distance. 'I'll go to the cafeteria and have something hot and filling, I think. I…need to get out of here for a while, and if I don't have a big meal I'll never get rid of this foggy feeling from the brandy and I'll be useless the whole afternoon.'

'Lucy, for heaven's sake, I'm not expecting you to come back to work!' Malcolm said. 'Get an early start on your weekend away.'

But she shook her head firmly. 'I was brought up on a farm. I know the importance of getting straight back on a horse after a fall. This situation is no different, and I can't afford to be scared about the patients.'

'Point taken.' He nodded. 'Still, don't hurry back from lunch, and enjoy every minute of your weekend.'

Lucy did. It was the first weekend in March, the sea was warm and the weather was gorgeous. Charlotte revelled in this wonderful new thing, the ocean, which she hadn't seen since she was two years old and couldn't remember at all. Lucy told neither her parents nor her daughter about the woman with the gun. This was made easier by the police having reported, after examining the gun on Friday afternoon, that although real and potentially deadly it hadn't been loaded.

'Which doesn't mean you can't press charges,' they'd told her.

But Lucy had been firm on that point, and they'd agreed that, even aside from the woman's physical condition, a hospital had been far more appropriate than a remand centre in this instance.

In the late afternoon, just before she'd been ready to leave for the day, Malcolm had reported that the woman's surgery had been safely and successfully completed. She'd still been in Recovery at that time, and was to be under heavy sedation with morphine for the next few days to deal with the pain, as well as broad-spectrum antibiotics to treat any remaining infection in the other leg.

After discharge from hospital, once the woman's mental condition had been stabilised, she would go to a rehabilitation centre for some weeks, where she would be fitted with a prosthesis and would learn how to manage her day-to-day life.

There had as yet been no further clues as to her real identity or where she'd obtained the gun, and the police continued to be involved as they investigated both these questions.

Lucy spent as little time thinking about it during the weekend as she possibly could. Instead, she swam in the surf with Charlotte and paddled with her in the tidal lake nearby. They ate ice cream and played deck quoits on Granny's and Grandad's front lawn. They helped with some gardening. Dad couldn't handle the exertion as he once had, though he never complained. Both Lucy and Charlotte were thoroughly spoiled with love.

And on Saturday evening after dinner, as she'd told Malcolm she would, Lucy took her long solitary walk, and found that she wasn't dwelling on Friday's terrifying incident, but on what had happened afterwards when Malcolm had asked her out.

I feel as if a door has opened for me, she thought. Opened just a crack, and there's some exotic landscape on the other side. What I can glimpse of it looks beautiful and wonderful, but what if that's a deception?

What if, just out of sight, the beauty ends and it all

looks grim and dreadful? Do I dare to take the risk and go through?

It wasn't until Sunday night, back home, that she made up her mind.

I can't close the door without at least opening it wider, she decided. That's not how I've lived life in the past, and I don't want to start doing it now.

Accordingly, she found a private moment with him on Monday morning and said to him, 'I'd like to spend an evening with you, Malcolm, if you haven't changed your mind?'

'I haven't,' he said. 'What's more, I have a very big-eyed, beseeching invitation from Ellie to Charlotte. Can she please, *please* come and play on Saturday afternoon?'

Lucy laughed. 'You have the intonation down perfectly! How could I say no?'

'And afterwards I can bring them back to your place, we can give them a quick dinner there, then Jenny or her daughter can come and babysit. It will save you getting a sitter of your own, and makes the logistics simpler.'

'It sounds perfect,' she agreed. 'I have a folding bed I can set up in Charlotte's room, and Ellie can stay the whole night, if she'd like to, rather than you having to wake her up to take her home.'

'I'll check,' he answered. 'It would be her first sleep-over, but I suspect I'll be the only one who has any fears about her missing me!'

With all of this arranged, the working week seemed to pass quickly, and Lucy had no private time with Malcolm. She didn't mind. She sensed that their working relationship had already gone about as far as it could go. Generally, they worked well together, understanding each other's needs with few words, the way any two experienced members of a medical team might have done.

Occasionally, there were some irritated exchanges, misunderstood instructions or a painful bump as they got in each other's way. Again, though, these were the sorts of things that could happen with anyone, and they were relaxed enough with each other to let the incidents slide at once, leaving no unpleasant aftertaste.

Only on Friday did she start to get a sense of antic-ipation building inside her. She didn't voice it aloud. Adults tended not to! But Charlotte wasn't nearly so restrained. 'Ellie day tomorrow, Ellie day tomorrow,' she sang over breakfast, adding unnecessarily, 'I'm *so* excited, Mummy, and so is Ellie. We've never had a sleep-over before. Well, last weekend at Granny and Grandad's, but that doesn't count, and Ellie hasn't even ever had that.'

'Not at her own grandparents'?'

'She doesn't have grandparents.'

'Doesn't she?'

Lucy remembered that Malcolm's mother had died some years ago, and that his father had been in poor health when she'd known him before. Bronwyn's par-ents had been cold, distant people. New Zealanders, they'd come over to spend two weeks with their dying daughter, but had told Malcolm, dry-eyed and with a very tight kind of anguish in their faces, that they didn't want to keep up any contact with him or with Ellie after Bronwyn's death. It would be 'too painful' and would 'only confuse the child'.

Malcolm had reported all this to Lucy one night after his in-laws' departure, clearly angry about it and not able to comprehend such an attitude. She could only assume now that Bronwyn's parents had kept to their decision, and that Malcolm had been too emotionally distant from them to challenge it on Ellie's behalf.

'I said she could come and have a sleep-over at my Granny and Grandad's soon. That would be OK, wouldn't it, Mummy?'

'I expect so,' Lucy answered automatically. She was still thinking about Malcolm, and only took in the meaning of Charlotte's words after she'd answered.

Oh, dear! Not quite a promise, but *almost*, and Charlotte would be bound to view it that way. Already, after only a few weeks, they were so strongly knitted into the fabric of Malcolm's and Ellie's lives. If her dinner with Malcolm tomorrow was a disaster...

She didn't try to think too much about the possible consequences.

The working day, fortunately, brought a good omen. It was exactly a week since the dramatic incident with the homeless woman and the gun, and Malcolm had been relaying any news he received about her condition to the rest of the staff in the department.

Physically, Alphonsine was doing well. The site of the amputation was healing as it should, and her course of antibiotics had eliminated the infection in her other leg. Mentally, she was still not making complete sense, although the medication she was on had calmed her, and she'd had two or three periods of moderate lucidity. She had spoken of someone called Mary, seeming upset that Mary wasn't there, but hadn't yet been able to explain who Mary was.

On Friday morning, however, Jean Jarrett took a phone call from a young woman, asking about emergency admissions. Had they treated anyone called Mary

Sisley? Or anyone who couldn't give her own name and who seemed confused or mentally ill?

'I transferred the call up to the surgical ward where they've got our friend La Comtesse,' Jean reported to the rest of the staff. She was a cheerful woman in her late fifties, who took a rather ghoulish but ultimately harmless interest in the unit's more dramatic cases.

'Do you know who the caller was?' Malcolm asked.

'Her niece, apparently. I didn't hear any further details.'

Two hours later the full story was revealed, when a young, pretty redhead in her early twenties came up to the reception desk, said her name was Mary Sisley Jones and asked if she could speak to Lucy and Malcolm in private in connection with her aunt, who had been calling herself Alphonsine de Crespigny.

'I'm so sorry about it all,' she said, once the three of them were closeted in Malcolm's office. 'What you must both have felt! May I tell you the full story?'

'Please, do,' Malcolm said.

'Auntie Mary was doing fine until six months ago, when my grandfather died. She'd been living with him for some years, and he always made sure she took her medication. She'd had to give up teaching—she was a French teacher, quite an inspirational one, as you might have gathered. But her mental health wasn't quite strong enough for that any more. She was happy and lucid most of the time, though, and largely in touch with reality.

'But then, as I said, Grandpa died. He was eighty-seven. She didn't cope too well, and it fell to me to deal with everything. She insisted on selling the house and all the furniture. She has all the money from the sale still in the bank! But I just couldn't get her to make any plans about the future, and I didn't know what to do.

'The house backs onto the nature reserve, and she set up a little camp there for herself in a wild gully on the slopes of Black Mountain. She always loved camping, and had all her own equipment. Technically, I suppose she was homeless.'

'Yes,' replied Malcolm. 'It was fairly obvious she'd been living rough.'

Her camp must have been quite close to his own house, which backed onto the Black Mountain reserve as well.

'But she seemed happy,' Mary Jones continued, 'and I let her stay there because the weather was warm, and I wondered if it was a way of dealing with her grief. She sometimes got angry if I came to visit her and she thought I was interfering, trying to get her to move into a flat or, heaven forbid, a hostel or halfway house, "pestering" her about her medication. So I'd just sort of wander past every couple of days, as if I was enjoying a walk in the bush, to check that she was all right.

'Then I got married a month ago. She wouldn't come to the wedding, and she said I was… Well, she called me all sorts of things and said she never wanted to see me again. *That's* when I should have insisted she get help, even if she wouldn't take it from me, even if it meant involving the police. Because she'd have kicked and screamed, I know, if anyone had tried to take her away!

'So I left it. I admit, I was angry, too! And frantic over the wedding, and buying a house. We've been on our honeymoon. We just got back yesterday. I went to check on her this morning, and her camp was wrecked. The old tent was all torn, and most of her gear had been stolen. I was terrified about what might have happened to her.

'And I was right, of course—she hadn't been taking her medication. Oh, I *shouldn't* have let her stay there on her own while I was away!'

'Do you know how her legs could have got so bad?' Malcolm asked. 'The infections, I mean.'

'Burns from her campfire? Scratches from the scrub? Who knows?'

'The amputation was the result of peripheral vascular disease, as you may have been told.'

'Yes, she's always smoked like a chimney. But I heard what happened, what she did when she came in here for treatment, and, of course, *that's* my fault, too. It was Grandpa's gun, and I knew he had it, but we couldn't find it when we dealt with all his things. Auntie Mary told me it was lost, but I should have known. At least she hadn't taken the bullets! I found them first and got rid of them, thank goodness!'

'Did her seeing you have any effect on her mental state?' Lucy asked.

The young woman's face brightened. 'Yes! She recognised me at once.'

'She'd been asking about someone called Mary, apparently,' Malcolm said.

'Yes, that's me. Mary Sisley Jones I am now. I was named after her, and I'm terribly fond of her. Silly! If I *hadn't* been so fond of her, I might have been tougher on her, but I really thought that her little camp up at the back of the house might be what she needed.'

'Perhaps it was, too, until she stopped taking her medication,' Malcolm suggested.

They talked for a few minutes longer. Mary didn't know yet what the future held for her aunt. 'I'd like to persuade her to come and live with Simon and me, but we can't make plans until she's fully stable. At least I've told Dr Nairn what drug and dosage worked best for her in the past, and he's confident she'll be in a better state soon.'

When she left, Malcolm commented to Lucy, 'Quite a contrast to how things looked for "La Comtesse" last Friday.'

'It is,' she agreed, 'and it makes me feel a lot better. I hate it when we have to deal with mental patients who are falling through a hole in the system.'

Malcolm paused by the open door of his office and said softly, 'Good, because I was hoping you'd be looking forward to tomorrow, not dwelling on last week.'

'I am looking forward to it,' she answered. 'Very much.'

They smiled at each other, and Lucy suddenly felt like bursting forth in a variation of Charlotte's song over breakfast this morning. 'Malcolm day tomorrow, Malcolm day tomorrow.'

At that moment, like a child, she couldn't imagine that their evening could possibly go wrong.

CHAPTER SIX

As AGREED, Lucy took Charlotte around to Malcolm's at two o'clock on Saturday afternoon.

It was a hot day, with a hazy sky and a hot north wind blowing. There was the acrid smell of smoke in the air, creating a sense of disquiet.

Despite the heat, Malcolm and Ellie were both in the garden at the side of the house, where the steep block of land had been levelled to provide an area for playing and sitting. Ellie was wearing her bathing suit and a sun hat, and was being permitted the messy luxury of having the hose running in her sandpit, while Malcolm tackled some gardening jobs. The rectangle of lawn was freshly mown, and over to one side he'd made a mound of prunings ready to be taken to the municipal composting depot.

He obviously hadn't deemed it necessary to dress up to receive her, Lucy thought, taking in the misshapen Akubra hat, the stained khaki shorts, a short-sleeved aertex shirt, which might once have been white, and a pair of hefty leather boots.

Should I mind? she asked herself, smoothing her own flowing and very summery pastel skirt.

Maybe she should but she couldn't!

Malcolm greeted her with a big, unselfconscious grin as he dumped another bundle of clippings on the pile with his gloved hands, and she wondered whether it was being a farmer's daughter, or whether it went further back. Surely it must be some primal, prehistoric impulse in a female to find a man so utterly attractive when he had dirt smeared on his bare, tanned, muscular legs and sweat sheening his lean, strong neck, and a primitive tool in his hand—in this instance, a pair of sharp, shiny secateurs.

'Hi, Charlotte. Hello, Lucy.' He came up to them, put the secateurs down on a convenient rock and threw his thick suede gardening gloves down beside them. 'Shall I take your backpack for you?' he said to Charlotte, and she nodded.

He bent and helped to ease the straps off her shoulders, then gave her a pat on the back and sent her off to Ellie.

'I've got my swimmers on underneath,' Charlotte told her friend, and promptly peeled off her dress and jumped into the waterlogged sandpit. In the space of a minute, she was as messy as Ellie.

'You're a brave man,' Lucy commented to Malcolm.

He knew at once what she meant. 'I'll hose them off when they're done,' he answered cheerfully. 'I'm assuming there's a change of clothes in her backpack in case of further disaster?'

'As per your instructions, yes.'

'I won't keep you, then,' Malcolm said. 'You've probably got things to do.'

'Er, yes,' Lucy replied quickly.

She was actually going to the shopping mall to try and buy a dress suitable for this evening, but didn't want to confess that fact. It suggested a degree of panic that she was reluctant to admit to, and hadn't fully explored in herself.

'Charlotte, watch that you don't get sand or water in your eyes, little mate,' Malcolm called. 'Ellie, don't wave the hose around like that, love. We might turn it off now that there are two of you. It's asking for trouble, isn't it?'

'I'll see you later on, Malcolm,' Lucy said.

But she didn't make a move just yet. Instead, she watched him as he went to turn off the hose. He was as easy and natural with Charlotte as he was with Ellie, and all at once, in the harsh, hot light, she could see the resemblance between them. It wasn't a question of colouring. He had grey eyes, while Charlotte's were blue. His hair was dark and rich in tone, while Charlotte's wasn't as fair as Ellie's but still qualified as blonde.

The similarity was much more one of gesture and attitude. It was from Malcolm that Charlotte got her determined jaw and chin, her sturdy build, her decisive way of moving and her sudden smile. He'd given her his high forehead, too. As Charlotte swept some wet and slightly sandy hair off her face with an equally wet and sandy hand, the similar shape of the bone structure was very obvious.

I haven't faced it until now, Lucy realised, as she drove to the mall. I haven't faced it at all. I'm going to have to tell him. It would be different if we'd just run into each other in the street, or something. Or even if we were simply working together, the way I work with Brian Smith or Heather Woodley. He needn't have known. It would probably be better for everyone if he didn't know.

But if he's going to start building a relationship with Charlotte as Ellie's best friend…and then there's this evening out together as well. I'm not sure what he wants from that. Friendship, judging by the way he put it last week, because I'm a link with Bronwyn and with Ellie's infancy. That's all.

The way she felt about him, such a friendship was horribly inadequate, and yet it would have to do.

But to build even a casual friendship when there was such a huge, vital truth that she was keeping from him would be impossible. She hadn't allowed herself to see this until now. She'd still wanted to protect him, to keep him from having to face the knowledge that their mistake of six years ago wasn't nearly as safely buried by time as he thought. It had a living consequence in the present.

And, as time went by, to keep this secret from him was no longer protection but betrayal.

Not yet, she decided. Think about how you're going to say it first at least. Don't muck it up. Maybe later tonight, when we've talked. Or maybe not. I won't plan it to that extent.

She managed to buy a dress, though her mind wasn't really focused on the task. Fortunately, the shops weren't crowded today, and an assistant came to her rescue and guided her to a silky, silvery-grey dress that suited her colouring and was just right in style, softly figure-hugging.

At home, she tidied the house a little, then rejected the idea of gardening. It really wasn't a pleasant day, with that wind and that smoky haze. She wondered where the fires were, and whether the weekend staff at the hospital were dealing with any fire-related casualties.

Happy to be indoors, she sat down for half an hour with iced coffee and a book, and was only just beginning to think about the girls' dinner when she heard a car in the driveway. They'd arrived early, quite a bit earlier than she'd been expecting.

She told Malcolm so quite cheerfully, expecting some

explanation involving the children, but he didn't comment, just said to Charlotte, 'Didn't you have something to show Ellie in your room? The birthday cake book?'

'That's not in my room. It's on the cookbook shelf.'

'Well, why don't you get it and take it into your room so you can show it to Ellie in peace and quiet?'

Malcolm seemed impatient and on edge, and eager to get her alone, she could tell. This impression was so strong that she turned to him as soon as the girls had gone and demanded of him, 'What is it, Malcolm? What's wrong?'

She saw the answer in his face even before he spoke. Her speculations about how to tell him the truth about Charlotte were irrelevant now. He already knew.

'I overheard Charlotte telling Ellie the date of her birthday,' he said. 'They were making pretend birthday cakes in the sandpit. Was she premature, Lucy?' The question seemed to hold a deliberate threat.

'No, she wasn't.'

She looked up at him unflinchingly, fully aware of how angry he was, and why.

'I didn't think so.' He took a couple of restless paces across the floor, his mood seeming to fill the room, then he rounded on her. 'Were you *ever* going to tell me?'

He was restraining his emotion, as if waiting until he was quite sure it was justified before he let fly.

'Not if we hadn't met up again the way we did,' she answered, instinctively knowing that he wanted the truth without embellishment or pretence.

'But we did meet up, weeks ago, and we're working together, and our daughters are friends. Friends!' he repeated harshly. 'Hell, they're half-sisters!'

'Yes.'

'And you've known it for six years and made no

attempt to track me down. Even for the past four weeks you've said nothing. You've actively let me believe Charlotte's father was that boy in Brewarra. The relationship that "didn't work out". Was there ever a boy at all, I wonder?'

'Yes, there was,' she answered. 'But when he found out I was pregnant—I told him straight away, not realising until I was almost three months along—he didn't want to know, and I couldn't blame him. He knew the baby wasn't his.'

'He knew a hell of a lot more than I did, then!'

'Malcolm—'

'You're going to explain?'

'I'm going to try to.'

'It had better be good.'

They were standing close together in the kitchen. Incongruously, Lucy had time to realise that they'd had some very emotional scenes together in kitchens in the past. He towered over her, and might have been menacing her if she hadn't trusted him so profoundly. She knew he would never be violent. She only hoped he'd be fair, and would understand.

'I don't know if it'll be *good*,' she told him. 'But it'll be the truth. That's all I can give you, Malcolm.'

'Fair enough,' he growled.

Still dressed in the clothes he'd worn out in the garden, he looked unkempt and fiery and gorgeous. She had to resist a strong impulse not to talk at all, just to reach up and tidy the hair off his forehead, remove a twig that was stuck to the shoulder of his shirt, then pillow her head on his chest so that she could hear his heartbeat and say, Can my explanation wait? Right now, I just want to hold you. It's so good that you know the truth at last. It's been such a burden…

But she knew that wouldn't satisfy him. Or her, when it came down to what really counted. Now that he knew Charlotte was his daughter, she wanted him to hear the full story.

Not that there was really a lot more to tell.

'I didn't even think about the fact that I might be pregnant after that night,' she said. 'All I could think about was how it must feel for you. I knew you wouldn't flinch from facing the knowledge that you'd betrayed Bronwyn, and I just wasn't going to hang around in your life for a second longer than necessary to remind you of it. You had enough to deal with—your grief, Ellie's fragility. I've told you all this—how I went straight to my parents' farm, and started going out with Brett McConnochie within a week. We…never slept together.'

'I guess that saved you from any guesswork!'

She ignored the biting aside. 'I had so much on my mind that I didn't take any notice of what was happening in my body. I just thought it was an irregular cycle, and any symptoms I put down to the stress of my time nursing Bronwyn and Ellie and the move back to Brewarra. When I realised, I knew straight away that I couldn't tell you. I was out of your life for ever, or so I thought, and I knew the only way you'd manage to put the whole thing behind you was if it could be limited to that one night. How would you have lived with yourself if you knew there'd been such a consequence? I wanted to spare you that, Malcolm, and even when our paths crossed again a few weeks ago, that was all I could think of at first—sparing you the pain of reliving it all.

'But when I saw you with Charlotte today in the garden… Something about that harsh light brought out similarities in your faces and bodies that I hadn't noticed...or hadn't allowed myself to see...until then. And the rapport you seemed to have with her, almost by instinct. It hit me like a blow in the stomach, and I knew I had to tell you. The only thing I hadn't worked out was when. I'm sorry you had to find out the way you did. It must have been a terrible shock.'

'For about ten seconds,' he acknowledged. 'And then it seemed so obvious that I felt like a fool for not having guessed before. You must have thought I was a fool.'

'No! No, Malcolm! Never that!'

He gave a frustrated sigh, and there was a silence as he wrestled with what she'd said. 'I believe you,' he told her finally. 'And you've taken the wind out of my sails.'

'That's good, isn't it?' she suggested tentatively.

'Is it?'

'Do you *want* to be angry with me, Malcolm?'

He spread his hands. 'I don't know what I want. There's been a huge earthquake in my world view. Charlotte is *my daughter*. I'm still reeling.'

She touched his arm, and he looked down at the place where skin met skin with a shocked expression, as if that one touch might set off an explosion. For several seconds they stayed like that, motionless, then he twisted his arm and slid his fingers in a light caress from her elbow to her wrist. Every hair on her body stood on end, and when he released her arm she instinctively hid it behind her back, like a naughty child.

'Look,' he said softly, 'I need to think. Things can't go on as before. Would it be all right if I left the girls here with you? I'll go home...and change...and have a couple of hours to myself, then come back here in time to go out as we arranged.'

'You can cancel that if you want to,' she offered. 'We could make up some excuse for Jenny and the girls.'

The awkwardness between them seemed to make the air prickle.

He shook his head. 'I don't want to cancel. We need to talk in a situation where there is no chance of them overhearing. Or anyone else, for that matter.'

'Go, then,' she agreed. 'Of course you can leave Ellie here. I was only going to feed them something very simple. It's not as if I need help in preparing it.'

'Then I'll see you in two hours. I'll bring Ellie's night things then.'

She was ready for him when he arrived, just after Jenny did, and she wasn't sorry that the baby sitter had got there first. She'd been on edge during every minute of the intervening two hours, and could only be thankful that the girls had been so happily absorbed in their play that they hadn't detected her mood.

She couldn't get Malcolm or his words out of her mind. He'd said he wanted to think, and that they'd need to talk over their meal, as if a strong inkling of what he wanted was already fixed in his mind.

Her own mind was ticking over at twice its normal speed, and she'd begun to have a clear suspicion about what he intended…which perhaps made the purchase of a new dress this afternoon particularly appropriate.

Viewing herself in the mirror after Jenny had opened the door and Lucy had heard Malcolm's voice in the hall, she was quietly pleased with what she saw. Knowing she was no great beauty, she was able to focus on the assets she did have—clear, peachy skin, wide green eyes, soft hair which obligingly allowed her to style it in several different ways. And the new silver-grey dress was definitely a success.

She came expectantly towards him along the corridor, hoping he would comment, but he didn't. He still looked miles away, and as if his thoughts were churning at the speed of light. Tall and easily dominating the space of the small hallway with the dark bulk of his suit, he moved restlessly as he talked with Jenny. Evidently he could hardly contain his impatience to leave.

'Both in bed by eight o'clock, Jenny,' he was saying. 'They've played pretty hard this afternoon.'

'Charlotte's toothbrush is ready in the bathroom,' Lucy added. 'And her nightie is laid out on the bed. The folding bed is set up for Ellie right next to Charlotte's. And I'm sure they'd both like a story, which is fine with me.'

'Go along then, you two,' Jenny said, her brown eyes twinkling. 'You sound as if you think I've never done this before.'

'I'll just kiss Charlotte goodnight,' Lucy murmured, self-conscious about the way Jenny's words had linked her to Malcolm.

'You two.' It was what you said to couples. The way she'd given each of them a pat on the back as she'd spoken only served to strengthen this impression.

Lucy's stomach turned over. To be a couple with Malcolm… She hardly dared to contemplate what that would mean after all this time.

He'd chosen a very expensive restaurant in the centre of the city, and when they were seated in a secluded corner table he commented on her appearance at last. 'You look great, Lucy. I'm glad I wore this suit, or I wouldn't have looked fit to be your escort.'

She laughed, and blushed a little, then murmured, 'I don't think you'd ever have much to fear on that score,

Malcolm, even if you were still in your gardening clothes.'

'No, I insist, it's the suit. Fine feathers make fine birds.'

'I have to admit, I do *not* think of you as a bird.'

He laughed, then they studied their menus in silence. Lucy finally chose a light pasta, knowing she probably wouldn't be able to eat much. Why was she feeling like this? So fluttery in the stomach. Did it make such a huge difference that he knew the truth about Charlotte now?

Yes! Yes, it did! The love that had burned in her six years ago, without her being aware of it until the very end, had never really gone away. The advent of Charlotte had kept its flame quietly burning, and now that Malcolm was so closely meshed in her life once more, that flame had flared even more brightly.

They talked about impersonal things as they ate. He had watched the news and weather at home before picking her up, and there were several fires burning around Canberra, with no hope of a change in the weather until Monday.

'I have my pager with me,' he said. 'It's possible I'll get called in.'

'Would your house ever be threatened?' she asked. 'You back onto the nature reserve, fairly near where Mary Sisley must have had her camp.'

'That's one of the reasons I was thinning out the shrubbery today,' he said. 'Less fuel for a fire to take hold of.'

They agreed that the danger wasn't great, and that her own house was safer still, surrounded as it was by other houses, rather than bushland.

Then he put down his knife and fork, making a little

clatter on the plate, and it seemed like a signal. Time to get down to business.

'Let's talk about what's really on our minds, Lucy,' he said quietly. His grey eyes seemed to burn into hers across the table. There was a white candle flickering in the middle of it, and she could see the dancing flame reflecting in his dark pupils. 'I've been thinking about nothing else,' he continued. 'And first I want to say that I think you're doing a wonderful job with her. She's a delightful little girl, bright and affectionate and curious and happy.'

'A little bossy!'

'A little bossy,' he agreed. 'She has spirit, and the confidence to be that way. Your parents must be great people, too.'

'Oh, they are.'

'I envy them... I envy you...for having seen her grow and change over those early years.'

'Malcolm, I know, I've deprived you of that, and if you—'

'You couldn't have done otherwise,' he cut in. 'It didn't take me long to realise that, as I thought about it today. Even if I'd known about her then, I couldn't have enjoyed her. It would have been a terrible situation. I can't even imagine how we could have got through the first few years of her life without damaging her—and ourselves—through guilt and hostility and regret. You were right in the decision you took back then, but now it's different, and I've got a proposition to make which I want you to think about very carefully.'

Lucy felt her heart begin to pound, and knew that her colour had heightened. Surely there was only one thing he could say which would merit such a preamble. And, loving him, she already knew what her answer would be.

She had even taken time to consider the biggest risk—that it wouldn't work because he didn't love her—and she'd decided that she had the courage and faith to take that risk with her eyes open, in the belief that if she loved him, he'd one day come to love her.

So, yes, she would marry him, and give Charlotte the father and sister that were rightfully hers.

'What I want to propose,' he said slowly, 'is that we tell the girls the truth—or as much of it as they'll understand at their age—as soon as possible. What do you think, Lucy? Is there a way we can do it? They deserve to know that they're sisters, don't they?'

It was like being doused in a bucket of icy water…to be followed by a burning sensation as she wondered feverishly how much her body language had betrayed about what she'd been thinking. She was leaning forward, her eyes were shining and she practically had the word 'yes' already formed on her lips. She would have felt like an utter fool if she hadn't felt so raw and hurt.

She looked down, and discovered that she was twisting the white linen table napkin in her hands, making it wet with the moisture from her palms. She knew he was waiting for her answer, some sort of measured response, exploring the best interests of the girls, suggesting a way to pitch the truth at a level they'd comprehend. But she couldn't answer him yet.

Oh, she *was* a fool! To have thought he'd suggest marriage, after what he'd been through. He'd *been* married, a love match, unencumbered by the past, or by children, or by ulterior reasons, and even that marriage, she knew, had been difficult and had required an enormous amount of work. Truly knowing the meaning of the words 'for better, for worse', Malcolm Lambert was the last man in the world who would suggest such a thing lightly.

She felt as if she had been catapulted back through the years to the most difficult moments in her pregnancy, to her painful twenty-two-hour labour and the hard, solitary work of delivery, to all the lonely moments when her parents' loving support still hadn't been quite enough. Back then, more than once, she'd indulged in a fantasy that Malcolm would track her down, come to Brewarra in search of her, sweep her into his strong arms and say, 'Marry me, Lucy. It's the only way to make something right come out of what we did.'

Oh, she'd wanted that so badly at times, even though she'd known in her heart that it couldn't happen.

'You haven't said anything,' Malcolm prompted.

'No, I—'

'Are you angry, Lucy? You look angry.'

She smiled vaguely and tried to make the brooding expression disappear from her face. She took a deep breath. 'Not angry. But I *don't* think we should tell them.'

'Why not?' It was a heated question. 'Why maintain the secrecy, and the pretence? Ultimately, I don't think that sort of dishonesty—'

'Do we have to call it that?' Her own heat was building now, too.

'It is dishonest, isn't it?'

'I suppose you've never let Ellie believe in Father Christmas or the tooth fairy, because that's dishonest, too.'

'Don't be ridiculous, Lucy. That sort of comparison is completely unfair.'

'Surely what's unfair is to burden them with a story

they can't really understand,' she replied hotly. 'How would we phrase it? Do we tell them the whole dreadful truth? What if it ruins their friendship? Being sisters would probably be a very romantic idea for them at first, but the bloom would wear off and then what are we all left with? Awkwardness. And no more real connection than we had in the first place.'

She was painfully aware that you couldn't make a true connection happen simply by *wanting* it. The intimate, explosive connection she'd had with Malcolm six years ago had produced the beloved miracle of Charlotte, but it had also produced many episodes of loneliness and pain, and it was these memories that were colouring her perception, and the tone of her voice, as she spoke.

'It seems a very *arid* solution to me, Malcolm,' she went on. 'To tell them, and then go on as before.'

She saw his face gradually close as her own words grew more and more intense, and when she'd finished he jumped in straight away. 'Arid? I don't see it as arid at all. Civilised, perhaps. Certainly *modern*. And I don't see what's so wrong in simply being civilised.'

'Civilised?' She laughed rather harshly. 'The beginning of this, six years ago, wasn't exactly civilised, was it?'

'No,' he agreed briefly. Their eyes met for a fraction of a second, then Lucy looked quickly down at the table, where she was still fiddling with her damp, incurably creased napkin. 'Does that make a difference?'

'It has to, doesn't it?' she returned. 'Think about it, Malcolm. How could we possibly explain it to them without bringing all that out? The only way I've managed to explain Charlotte's lack of a daddy to her until now has been by being very, very vague. How can we suddenly announce that she *does* have a daddy, and it's you, and therefore Ellie is her sister, when they both already know that Ellie's mother is dead? I...' She shook her head, then finished firmly, 'I won't do it, Malcolm. Not yet.'

He nodded slowly. 'I see your point of view. I don't agree with it. I think there are other considerations. But I can't force the issue, can I? It has to be agreed between us first, before we take any action. And you've exercised your power of veto. I have to accept that.'

He was silent for quite a while, and now *he* was the one staring down. She watched him, and was shocked at the bleakness she saw in his face. As in the past, it brought a surge of tenderness in her, and a deep need to reach across and smooth away the tension with her fingers. And her lips.

'You talked about other considerations, Malcolm,' she said desperately.

He looked up. 'Not for you, I expect. You're rather well provided for, when it comes to family.'

'What do you mean?'

'Well, you *have* one. Ellie and I don't. Charlotte has loving grandparents who she's utterly familiar and at home with. She has an aunt, doesn't she? Your sister?'

'Yes, and three cousins, slightly older. She adores them. They'll probably come down for a visit soon.'

'You see what I mean? Family. You don't know what a blessed luxury that is. My parents are dead, as you probably know, and I don't know if you remember Bronwyn's parents, and what they were like?'

'Yes, I do.'

'Both of us were only children. That was one of the things we had in common at first, but now it means that Ellie has no one but me.'

'I understand, Malcolm.'

'But you think I'm trying to provide her with an instant family, and you don't think it will work.'

'Something like that. I suppose I've seen that it *doesn't*, always. Please, let's think for longer about this before we do anything rash.'

He nodded once more, and this time it seemed as if there was nothing further to say.

'Dessert?' he prompted her, once their empty plates had been taken away.

'I couldn't, tonight.'

'No appetite?'

'Not really.'

'I'll ask for the bill next time the waiter appears, then. Feelings are a pretty powerful appetite-suppressant, aren't they? I lost a lot of weight after Bronny died.'

'Surely you didn't have a lot to lose?'

'I didn't,' he agreed. 'A colleague in Brisbane had to point out the truth to me in the end. That I wouldn't be much use to Ellie if I didn't maintain my own health. So I started eating properly again, and I joined a gym and took up swimming. I'm fitter these days than I was in my teens, because I was rather a weed until Bronwyn got hold of me.'

She laughed. 'What an extraordinary choice of words, Malcolm! You can't possibly have been ''a weed''! And did Bronwyn really ''get hold of you''?'

Strange. They'd been on the point of leaving, but instead they stayed for another hour, drinking three cups of coffee each and eating the delicate dark chocolates that appeared at the same time without even noticing them. Mostly, they talked about Malcolm's marriage, in an intimate, searching way that was only possible because six years had gone by.

While saying nothing disloyal about his wife, Malcolm sketched a vivid picture of the complexity and shifting balances in their relationship. Bronwyn had been the strong one at first, a year older than Malcolm and possessing a tough carapace built by her over-disciplined childhood in which parental love had been expressed through endless rules and super-high expectations.

Malcolm's childhood had prepared him differently for adult life. His elderly parents, kind and loving but very out of touch, had taught him a huge amount about being sensitive to the needs of old people, being kind to helpless creatures, appreciating art and music and nature, but very little about the rough and tumble of friendship with contemporaries, about healthy competition, goal-setting and determination.

At the beginning of their relationship Bronwyn had lectured him, yelled at him, goaded him into proving himself, until he'd discovered how to use his rich inner resources to achieve success on his own, while she had burned herself out and become a little lost. She had failed her final law exams, tried to start her own clothing design business and finally told him, 'I need a baby, Malcolm. That's what this is all about. Being a parent will give me direction again, I know it, and everything will fall into place.'

Malcolm had believed that she'd been right. She'd had a huge amount of love to give, if only she could have learned to give it tenderly, not imperiously and always seeking an impossible degree of control. They'd both been ecstatic over Ellie's conception, but then... Well, Lucy knew the rest, and knew how Bronwyn had fought powerlessly for control until almost the end.

'I was exhausted,' Malcolm finished. 'Utterly exhausted. At first, she was the one who taught me, but by the end that had reversed and I was battling, *battling* to teach her some of the things I knew about acceptance and peace, and, dear Lord, she was the most difficult, recalcitrant, combative student you can possibly imagine. You had to love her for it, or admire—*value*—her for it, even when you were ready to yell and stomp and *throw* things in frustration.'

He shook his head. Then he added helplessly, 'Sorry. Are your ears falling off?'

She grinned and reached her fingers up as if to test them. 'A bit loose, but I think they'll stay put.'

'What's the time?' He looked at his watch. 'No! Oh, Lucy, I really *am* sorry!'

'Don't be,' she said lightly. 'I'll tell you about my life one day, and then we'll be even.'

She didn't want to admit to him just how precious the past hour had been, and how important in freeing her from the tangled chains of the past. For over six years she'd had questions and conjectures about Malcolm's relationship with Bronny. Now she was free from those. She knew the truth, as Malcolm saw it, and it felt like a new beginning.

He must have felt that way, too. As they drove back to her place through the thick night, he said to her, 'Well, I've apologised. Now I'm going to thank you.'

'For—?'

'For listening the way you did. I'd said some of this to my friend Adam several years ago, but he's in Alice Springs now, and we haven't seen each other for a while. As I've acquired a greater distance and better perception, there's been no one to share it with. Till you. And you were the right person, Lucy.'

'I— Well, I'm glad. Happy to be of service.' She

used the polite cliché deliberately, still wanting to keep a little distance between them.

Odd creatures we women are, she thought. I'm so glad he chose to confide in me, but if that's the only way he thinks of me, as some kind of agony aunt, oh, that's mortifying, and not what I want from him at all!

CHAPTER SEVEN

A FEW minutes later, Malcolm turned his car into Lucy's drive and switched off the engine.

'Mind if I come in with you?' he said. 'I want to hear a report from Jenny, and creep in to have a look at Ellie before I head off.'

'Of course you must come in,' Lucy told him. 'I'd even offer you more coffee, except that we're already swimming in it, aren't we?''

'No, no coffee,' he agreed. 'A glass of water, maybe. My throat is very dry. You can really smell the smoke in the air, can't you?'

'Yes, there's always something ominous about it in summer, so different from the smell of bonfires on the Queen's Birthday weekend in June,' she answered.

'The wind has dropped for now, which must be helping the bushfire brigades, but I expect it will pick up again in the morning. I'll ring the hospital when I get home and see if they've had any casualties brought in.'

Jenny commented on the smoke in the air as well. 'The girls were a little anxious. I explained that it was the wind blowing the smoke over, and the fires weren't as close to us as they seemed.'

'Thanks, Jenny,' Malcolm said. 'Head off now, while we check on the girls. Make sure you write down the extra hours because I'm bound to lose track.'

'Don't worry, Dr Lambert.'

She said goodnight, and they heard her car start out in the street a minute later as they crept down the corridor to Charlotte's room. Ellie seemed to be having a nightmare. Although lying still, she was making a steady stream of groaning sounds in her sleep.

Malcolm explained in a whisper as he caught Lucy's alarmed look, 'She often does that. I don't know why. It may be the legacy of her asthma, which has tapered off a lot over the past year. I'll try rolling her over. That sometimes makes her stop.'

He bent down and gently turned her from her back to her side, and she did quieten and begin breathing peacefully again.

Lucy tiptoed between the beds, kissed Charlotte and brushed the mass of fair hair off her face. Then they both left the room again. At the front door, Lucy recalled, 'You wanted a glass of water.'

'It doesn't matter. I'll grab one at home.'

But he didn't move. Lucy already had her fingers on the doorknob, ready to open it, but something about the way he was looking at her made her freeze, the action uncompleted.

'Tonight, when we talked,' he began, then amended quickly, 'No, when *I* talked. Did you feel used, Lucy?'

'No.' She shook her head, while meeting his gaze steadily. She knew that colour was beginning to flood into her cheeks, but didn't care if he saw it.

'Good.'

She thought about trying to explain what she *had* felt, then didn't have the courage. She didn't fully understand the conflicting feelings herself, and couldn't expect him to.

He was saying something else. 'Because I wasn't using you. I needed to say all that, but only because— Hell! Maybe I should just…'

He didn't finish. Instead, he just reached out and

pulled her against him, slowly enough that she could have pulled away if she'd wanted to, but, of course, she didn't. It was like heaven to be in his arms, like heaven to feel his mouth brush hers, then cling there and kiss her with such thoroughness that she was soon breathless and aching.

The tortured chemistry between them hadn't gone away. It had simply changed, with time, into something richer and freer and not tortured at all. She didn't have to cry about it any more—cry because it was wrong and yet he needed it so desperately that she had to give it to him.

There was nothing to cry about now. She could relish every tingling touch of his fingers along her jaw and through her hair, every press of his thighs against her. She could feel herself enveloped in his warmth and scent and knew, deep down, that she belonged there.

She wasn't thinking yet about how far it would go, although the future did suddenly seem to have taken on a beautiful pinkish hue. Beyond that, though, there was no urgency tonight. Time didn't matter. They could stand there for hours, exploring each other like teenagers, hungry for every fresh sensation. Amazing what lips could do! Wonderful how warm and strong a male body felt!

'Lucy, oh, Lucy,' Malcolm groaned. 'I didn't know that it would feel like this. So *simple*, now. So gloriously good and *simple*.'

Except that it wasn't really simple.

'Mummy! Mummy?' said a sleepy little voice, as bare feet came padding along the polished wood of the corridor. 'Mummy, Ellie was making noises in her sleep and it woke me up, but she's stopped now. What are you doing? Who is that man?'

They wrenched abruptly apart and stood there, staring at Charlotte, both of them breathless and unable to see properly. The light was on in the living room, and it came shafting through the open doorway so that they had to peer beyond it to see Charlotte's nightgown-clad figure emerging.

'It's…it's Ellie's dad, love,' Lucy managed.

'But you were kissing him.'

'Yes, I—'

'Like in *Beauty and the Beast*, when the beast turns into a prince and he kisses Belle.'

'Yes, I suppose it was a bit like that, wasn't it?'

Lucy was still having to fight to make her breathing sound normal, and was sure that no Disney kiss ever revealed the full reality of mussed hair, smudged lipstick, hectic cheeks and clothing in disarray.

'Does that mean you're going to get married?'

The innocent question rang in Malcolm's ears like a taunt, and he heard Lucy gasp and then groan under her breath.

He struggled to find words that wouldn't promise too much to Charlotte, but wouldn't dismiss what had just happened with Lucy. Yes, it had been a kiss, a passionate, fabulous, earth-shattering kiss, but…but…

Oh, Lord, he wasn't ready to think about marriage again yet, despite the conversation he'd had about it with Ellie recently. He suddenly understood why he'd felt compelled to bring up the subject with his daughter. At some deep, hidden level, he'd been very much hoping she would say no.

Not that he'd have dedicated himself to a lifetime of celibacy because of a six-year-old child's abstract and casually thought-out preference. But it would definitely have given him the excuse to postpone thinking about it for a bit longer.

He was deeply drawn to Lucy. Not just physically, but mentally and emotionally, too. There was a vast distance, though, between attraction, no matter how broad and sincere, and marriage. His marriage to Bronwyn had engulfed and consumed him. He'd tried to talk about this to Lucy tonight, and she had seemed to understand. He knew she hadn't expected him to kiss her. Her surprise and pleasure when he had, and her immediate response, had turned up the heat inside him by at least twenty degrees.

But now Charlotte's innocent question had confronted him with the fact that for most people it was... Well, there was a song about it, wasn't there? Something about love and marriage go together like a— No one even *drove* horses and carriages any more, but everyone still expected attraction to lead to a kiss, a kiss to lead to bed, bed to lead to love and love to marriage. Not necessarily in that order but, whichever order it was in, it was about three steps beyond where he wanted to take it, or even *think* about taking it, at this point.

He felt as if he were drowning, and his brain came up for air long enough to hear Lucy saying, 'No, Charlotte, love, it doesn't mean we're going to get married.' It had been said in a strangled, panicky sort of tone, which he might have laughed at if he hadn't known just how vital it was to navigate through this emotional minefield Charlotte had unwittingly created, without it blowing up in all of their faces.

It would be disastrous to laugh at Lucy now.

'Your mum was just giving me a goodnight kiss,' he told her cheerfully. 'Big people do that sometimes.'

'Only when they're going to get married,' Charlotte insisted. 'Otherwise it's not *nearly* such a big kiss.'

'Charlotte, let's get you back to bed, love,' Lucy said brightly. 'Do you need to pop to the loo?'

'No.'

'Well, I think we will, anyway.'

Charlotte began to cry. 'I don't want to go to the loo. I want you to marry Ellie's daddy. I *want* you to!'

'Charlotte...' Lucy began helplessly, not sure whether to try and soothe this stubborn mood away or be angry about it. Her daughter didn't usually wake up in the night like this, and all out of sorts to boot.

On a sudden intuition, she reached out to touch Charlotte's forehead. Definitely hot.

She turned to Malcolm, who looked as helpless and embarrassed as she felt. Possibly more so. 'I think she's getting a virus or an ear infection or something,' she said. 'Do your ears hurt, love?'

'No.'

'But you do feel feverish.'

'Is she very hot?' Malcolm said, coming forward.

'No, not in my judgement. You have a feel, Malcolm.'

'Feverish, but not serious, I think,' he said quietly. Charlotte was clutching Lucy's dress now, with big, glittering eyes fixed on Malcolm. 'Give her some medicine and— Look, I'll take Ellie home, I think,' he mouthed. 'You don't need to have her here if Charlotte's going to give you a bad night.'

'Better wait until she's dropped off again,' Lucy mouthed back. 'Or we'll have more tears.'

But in the end it wasn't an issue. Charlotte was persuaded to visit the toilet, and then adjourn to the bathroom for some 'red medicine', which she quite liked the taste of, fortunately. Then Lucy carried her back to bed, and the hot little head was lolling heavily on her shoulder before they even reached the bedroom.

After tucking her under the sheet, Lucy stood back while Malcolm scooped up Ellie, sheet, light blanket and all, and carried her along the corridor to the front door. She was still fast asleep.

'Uh…' he began after Lucy had ducked ahead of him to open the door.

But there was really nothing safe to say at this point. Instead, they both laughed ruefully, then shrugged and managed words of farewell.

'Oh, Charlotte,' Lucy sighed to her sleeping daughter a few minutes later as she went in to check on her one final time. 'I should thank you, shouldn't I? I've never seen a man look so hunted and so horrified at the mention of one simple word, and, of course, it's best to know at once where I stand.

'I knew it, deep down, anyway, after everything he said—and didn't say—tonight. In other words, I'm so far from standing beside him at the altar that I'm not even within sight of the church. But, I admit, I would rather have gone on with the illusion for a little longer, rather than having it shattered in such an embarrassing way, my innocent, gorgeous sweetheart.'

She bent down and gave Charlotte a last kiss, then took herself off to bed and spent a restless night.

Lucy didn't need to study the bleary faces of the night staff going off work on Monday morning to know that it had been a difficult shift.

The ever-thickening haze of smoke, the unrelenting heat and persistent wind and the voice of the newsreader on the radio this morning all told the same story. There were major fires near the town of Braidwood, in the Brindabella Ranges, and in Stromlo Forest, with at least one of the fires having been deliberately lit.

To anyone who'd ever lived on a farm or had had to deal with bushfire-related casualties—and Lucy had done both—the idea was appalling. Fortunately, the Stromlo Forest fire was now under control and wouldn't spread to threaten the city, but the weather still hadn't changed, and Black Mountain Hospital's Accident and Emergency department had received seven injured fire-fighters overnight, after a wall of fire had blown back on them, as well as four more the previous day. Lucy learned that Malcolm had worked most of Sunday and had been at the hospital all Sunday night.

The first of today's casualties had been treated for minor burns, smoke inhalation and a broken leg, and had now been transferred to the orthopaedic ward, but the others, admitted just half an hour earlier, were more seriously injured and not yet stable enough to be moved to the hospital's burns unit. In addition, the smoky air hanging over the city had triggered asthma and other respiratory complaints in many people, some of whom required hospitalisation to get their condition under control.

With her counterpart on the night-shift, Mark Conrad, staying only long enough to get her up to speed on volunteer firefighter Kim Turner's status, Lucy was immediately plunged into a working day so absorbing that she didn't manage to eat at all at lunchtime. All she had time for was a quick phone call to the school to ascertain that Charlotte was as well as she'd seemed that morning, and that her illness the previous day had really only been a twenty-four-hour virus.

Kim Turner, in contrast, hovered dangerously close

to death. He had suffered burns to his face and arms, as well as severe smoke inhalation and dehydration, and they had to work over him for a long time, setting up oxygen equipment for his breathing, starting an IV line for fluids and pain medication, dressing his burns and battling for his life for hours until it finally seemed possible that he'd pull through.

He still had a long road ahead of him, however, and would spend weeks in the small and very specialised burns unit that formed part of the hospital's intensive care ward.

Meanwhile, the news had come through that there was fire on Black Mountain itself, and it was spreading, though not out of control. This only added to the urgency in the atmosphere, for Malcolm as well as for everyone else.

'I hope they're happy with what we've done,' Lucy heard him comment tightly in reference to Kim Turner, an hour after he'd handed their patient over to the burns unit team. 'He had a massive shock to his whole system and it was a real balancing act to get his treatment right. I know Gil Henderson isn't in favour of—'

'Don't keep thinking about it,' Heather Woodley interrupted. 'Go home, Malcolm,' she ordered, just as Lucy was handing over to the nurse who'd just come on for the evening shift.

'And there are two others waiting for beds,' Lucy ended her summary, having to force her concentration. 'But you won't be concerned with those, other than stubbing your toes on their trolley wheels in the corridor as you go past.'

'That kind of a day, huh?' said Noelle Burnford sympathetically.

'Yes, and the weather still hasn't broken, though I'm

sure they said on the forecast this morning that a change was due.'

She wasn't really fully focused on what she was saying. Heather and Malcolm were standing just a few feet away, and she couldn't help noticing the possessive caress in Heather's tone as she lectured him, 'You *know* you're worried. About Ellie, and about your house. And we'll all understand if you need to go now. None of the rest of us live close enough to Black Mountain to be threatened, and the hospital itself has two suburbs and a four-lane main road between it and the fire, so there's no danger there. But *you...*'

Malcolm raked a tired hand through his hair as he began to walk down the corridor, with Heather still at his side. Lucy was walking just behind them.

'All right, then,' he conceded finally. 'I *am* concerned, of course. Not about Ellie's safety. I'm sure Jenny would leave the house if there was any danger. And, of course, everyone may be asked to evacuate, to be on the safe side. But Ellie is probably scared...worried about the cat...and the smoke could well trigger an asthma attack. Again, Jenny can handle it, but I'd like to be there.'

'Of course,' Heather soothed him. 'Would you like me to drop over with some take-aways tonight after I finish? I'm due to go off at sevenish.'

'No, thanks, Heather. You'll be far too tired yourself by that time to want to be rushing over to my place,' he answered, apparently just as concerned for her well-being as she was for his.

'Really, it'll be no trouble,' she insisted eagerly.

'I'm sure it wouldn't, but, please, don't.' This time Malcolm's real meaning was clearer—to Lucy, at least. He honestly didn't want Heather to come.

But Lucy was dismayed at the way her heart suddenly lifted.

Just because he's not interested in Heather Woodley, it doesn't mean he *is* interested in me, she reminded herself. It's pointless to go around viewing every other woman in his orbit with suspicion. If that kiss on Saturday was just a mistake, and he doesn't want to pursue it any further, the reason lies far more deeply inside him, and in the past, than that.

'Bye, Lucy,' he said as they started to go to different sections of the car park. Heather was still at his side, and echoed his goodbye.

Lucy answered both of them as politeness demanded, and could still hear Heather chatting away in a deter-mined fashion for another thirty seconds as their paths diverged.

The last thing she heard was, 'I know it's none of my business, but you really don't look after yourself as well as you should.'

At after-school care, Lucy found Charlotte hopping up and down, impatient to leave. 'Mrs Girdlestone says there's a fire on Black Mountain,' she said, 'right near where Ellie lives. We have to go round there and tell her, so she can escape.'

'I'm sure she knows about the fire already, and isn't in any danger, love,' Lucy said soothingly.

But Charlotte was tearfully insistent, to the point where Lucy put a hand to her daughter's forehead again. No, she seemed quite cool—or as cool as was normal on a dry-roasted day like this—and she didn't show any of the listlessness which had coloured her behaviour for most of yesterday.

'Do you feel well, Charlotte?' Lucy asked all the same.

'Yes, but I want to go and help Ellie look for the cat. Mrs Girdlestone says cats often go missing when there's a fire, and Ellie and I couldn't *bear* it if Pioneer got burned to death.'

Lucy sighed. She didn't normally allow herself to be pestered into action by her daughter, but on this occasion she had to admit to herself, It's exactly what *I* want to do, as well—go round to Malcolm's just in case there's something I can do. If they're being told to evacuate, or something, he and Ellie might want to stay with us.

She ignored the many obvious dangers inherent in this possibility and said aloud to Charlotte, 'Let's go home and change first, shall we?'

'Do you mean we *are* going?'

Again, Lucy sighed. 'Yes.'

'Oh, Ellie will be so glad. She really *needs* me, Mummy. I wish you could grasp that fact.'

Good heavens! Lucy stifled a laugh at the pompous choice of words. Charlotte frequently came out with gems of this sort. She had a retentive memory for adult conversation, and liked to practise phrases she'd heard. Lucy suspected that the school principal, Mr Halifax, was the culprit in this case.

At home, they ate a snack of fruit and iced chocolate, then changed quickly. Lucy insisted on long pants for both of them, just in case there was any question of tramping through the long grass and scratchy bush that sloped up from the back of Ellie's and Malcolm's house in search of the cat.

When they got there at a quarter to five, however, they found Pioneer safely shut indoors and no suggestion of an evacuation yet, although a yellow bushfire service vehicle was grinding its way along the back of the houses with a bulldozer in its wake, scraping a fire-break of raw brown earth.

The four of them went out to the gate in the back fence to watch, and a suited firefighter came up to them and told them, as he'd told several neighbours along the route, 'Stand by for any information. We're going house to house at the moment, telling people to fill up their baths and hose their wooden decks and back gardens. Close your windows facing the fire, and open the ones away from the fire. Keep your pets inside.'

'Yes, we've got the cat already.'

'The southerly change has hit Victoria, with some good rain. It should be here in a few hours. At the moment it's moving faster than the fire, and we have the front of the fire pretty well controlled. But if the wind picks up just ahead of the change, we may find it gets around us and it might get this far.'

Malcolm nodded. 'Stay put, then?'

'Yes, and get your hose ready.'

'What about the water pressure?'

'There aren't too many houses backing onto Black Mountain, so the system should be able to take it.'

'There you go, Charlotte,' Lucy told her daughter. 'We didn't need to worry after all. We can go home.'

Wrong.

'I can't leave Ellie in danger!' Charlotte said theatrically. 'I *need* to protect her.'

'No, you don't!' Ellie said indignantly. '*I* need to protect *you* because I'm older!'

'But I'm bigger.''

'So?'

'*And* you sound wheezy!'

'I just had my inhaler, and Daddy checked me and

said I'm fine. I *never* get really bad asthma any more since I started swimming a lot.'

'Anyway, the point is, we need to protect each other, so we can't go home yet. I'm sorry, Mummy.'

Malcolm was laughing. It was a lovely sound, rich and warm, with no hint in it of the complicated pain of his past. 'Stay if you like,' he told Lucy, his fingers running in a quick caress down her bare arm. 'In fact, *please*, stay!'

'But you told Heather—'

'You're *not* Heather.'

'Oh. No. I suppose I'm not,' she replied meekly, wishing her heart wasn't singing quite so loudly, and well aware of the significant look the two girls had just exchanged when they'd seen Malcolm touch her.

Charlotte had obviously relayed the whole story of that late-night, Beauty-and-the-Beast kiss at school to-day, with attendant speculations on the subject of marriage. Oh, dear…

They stayed for another three hours, and Lucy conceded to Malcolm halfway through it, 'This is rather fun.'

'In a dangerous kind of way.'

He meant the fire, she hoped.

The situation had hotted up as the wind had increased, and the fire had burned out the powerlines that serviced the area, so they got take-away pizza and ate it on the lawn as darkness fell. They could actually see the line of flame up on the slopes of Black Mountain, several hundred metres off, and hear the shouts of fire-fighters and the noise of truck engines grinding through the bush.

Then, just as it was completely dark, another of the

yellow emergency vehicles came toiling along the new fire-break, stopping at each house.

'All occupants accounted for?' they wanted to know. 'Is there anyone who has a teenager, perhaps, who isn't home yet? We really need to know if everyone in the houses along here is safe, and if there are any kids who play a lot up the back there, we'd like to talk to them.'

'What's happened?' Malcolm asked. Lucy could tell that his instincts had been alerted. This wasn't simply a routine question. 'Has a body been found?'

Lucy looked over towards the girls. They were still playing hide and seek in the garden, their mood very wild under the influence of all the excitement. But Malcolm's words had reminded her that the danger was real, and she didn't want the two little ones to be confronted too closely by the shocking possibility of death.

'No...' To her relief, the emergency worker shook his head. 'Nothing like that, thank goodness. And my men are all OK so far. But we've found the remnants of a camp up in a gully where the fire passed through. There would have been a lot of heat at that point because the trees were pretty dense. We're trying to find out if it was just kids who made the camp, or if someone was living there.'

'Mary Sisley,' said Lucy and Malcolm in unison at once.

'Then you know something about it?'

'The camp was abandoned,' Malcolm told the man. 'It was made by a homeless, mentally ill woman who came in to us as a patient. I'm the director of emergency medicine at Black Mountain. She's still in hospital. Her medication is almost back under control, and she'll be living with her niece once she's discharged. So I don't think you need to worry, unless there were signs of more recent occupation by someone else.'

'Can't tell.' He shook his head. 'But I expect not. It was a pretty out-of-the-way spot.'

'Which was why she chose it,' Lucy murmured to Malcolm after the emergency worker and his vehicle had passed on. She shivered slightly. 'Imagine if she'd still been there, if this had happened during that first spell of bushfire weather a few weeks ago while her niece was away on her honeymoon. I doubt very much if she'd have been able to get away in time. She'd have been burned to death.'

'It's an ill wind,' Malcolm agreed. 'She lost a leg, but she didn't lose her life. And speaking of the wind…'

They both felt it, a new freshness in the air and the smell of rain. There was lightning in the distance, too. The thunderstorm ahead of the change hit a few minutes later, and the rain came pelting down like liquid mercy in huge, cold drops. Racing for the car, Lucy and Charlotte got drenched, and they were even more drenched by the short trip from the carport to the front door at home.

Lucy put Charlotte into a warm bath at once, washed her hair to get rid of the smell of the smoke and had her tucked up in bed twenty minutes later. She'd just bent to give her daughter a goodnight kiss when Charlotte looked up at her with guileless blue eyes and said in an extremely unconvincing fashion, 'Oh, dear, Mummy, I just remembered. I left Debbie—I mean Debradoria Santafloria—at Ellie's place.'

'You left— Charlotte, I didn't even know you'd *taken* her!'

'No, well, I did, and I left her there. It was an accident. And you'll have to go and get her tonight because I need her for tomorrow at school.'

'Debbie?'

'Debradoria—'

'Yes, OK, but you need Debradoria Santafloria at *school*?'

'It's "Bring your favourite cuddly toy" day.'

'Oh.'

'So…'

'No!'

'Mummy-y-y!'

'Charlotte, how can I possibly leave you alone in the house at night to go back in the pelting rain and thunder to get your doll? I can't, and I'm not going to.'

'But—'

'What I *will* do…' What I'll have to do, although I really don't want to, and I have the strongest suspicion I'm being conned here! 'Is ring Ellie's dad and ask him to make sure that Ellie brings it in her backpack to school tomorrow for you.'

So she did, although if either she or Malcolm had realised at the time what a dangerous precedent they were setting…

CHAPTER EIGHT

'ARE we going to put a stop to this?' Malcolm asked.

He had appeared at the door on a Saturday morning at eight o'clock with Charlotte's home-reading folder in his hands. Thanking her lucky stars that she was now dressed, as she hadn't been five minutes earlier, Lucy gave a rueful shrug.

'I'm not sure that we can,' she answered him. 'They're cunning little creatures, even though they're so obvious about it. You and I both know that Charlotte left her folder at your place on purpose yesterday—'

'Yes, but I didn't want to call her bluff on it without consulting you,' he acknowledged, 'because I'm sure you want Charlotte to do her reading homework, and they're not seeing each other this weekend for one reason and another.'

'I wonder what they think they're going to achieve?'

'Isn't it obvious?' he drawled. His eyes swept over her and she could read them very easily.

She blushed and nervously brushed a strand of hair behind her ear. 'Yes, but do they think that forcing us to spend an extra two minutes in conversation while we return or retrieve all these left items is really going to deepen our relationship that much?'

'Lucy, they don't care about depth!' he pointed out with a touch of impatience. 'They're going by the stick system, not the carrot. They're trying to show us that it's such an incredible nuisance for the four of us to live apart that we really ought to live together.'

'I see. Of course.' She nodded. 'I'm obviously not quite as in touch with the kindergarten mentality as you are. Oh! That sounded like an insult, Malcolm, and I didn't mean it to.'

'I know,' he said, then added softly, 'I think I'm confident enough about the state of our relationship at this point not to suspect you of wanting to insult me.'

'I'm glad…'

'In fact, I'm wondering if the best way to get the dear little monsters off our backs is to— Damn! This isn't the right moment, is it?'

They'd both just heard Charlotte intoning rather persistently in the background, 'Mum-my! M-u-u-mmy!'

'Are you off to work?' Lucy questioned brightly instead, noting the way he was dressed. Tailored pants, a cream shirt, a fresh shave, in contrast to her own casual denim and cotton knit. She could still smell his aftershave, and it was fabulous.

'Yes, there was a gap in the roster, and I'll probably be on till late. Ellie is going on a picnic with Jenny and her family. But let me finish, Lucy.'

'M-u-u-mmy.'

'Am I the one who's preventing you?' she murmured drily.

'Yes, because any minute you're going to make the fatal mistake of *answering* that little voice, and then she'll know where you are, and— So I'm *not* going to waste any more time! I wanted to ask if you'd like to go out again,' he finished, rapid and determined. They could hear footsteps in the living room, heading their way.

'Yes, I would,' she answered urgently. 'Very much.'

'I'll ring you. It seems like the phone probably offers

us the greatest peace and privacy!' He was already half-way down the steps.

Charlotte frowned after him. 'Did he bring back my reading folder?'

'Yes, and it's the last time either of us is going to return the things you and Ellie leave at each other's houses, Charlotte. Is that clear?' Lucy said sternly. 'You both have to take more care.'

'OK, Mummy…' She sighed resignedly.

They both watched Malcolm as he got into his car, gave a brief wave and drove away. Then Charlotte said in a tone of gentle accusation, 'You really should have invited him in for a cup of tea or coffee, you know.'

Lucy recognised the tone as one she'd used herself with Charlotte many times, so it probably wasn't fair to criticise it. 'He had to go to work,' she explained.

'But he's the boss. He can be late if he likes.'

'Well, Charlotte, no, that's not really how it works…'

All in all, it was a long weekend, made longer, Lucy knew, by the fact that she couldn't help waiting for Malcolm to phone as he'd said he would.

His call finally came on Sunday night. 'I was going to ask you for dinner and a movie next Saturday, but Ellie informs me that she and I have both been invited down to "meet Granny and Grandad" next weekend. I'm sorry, the etiquette is delicate here, but I have to get it sorted out. Is this something you knew about? Something you planned to—?'

He broke off as Lucy's horrified gasp told him what he needed to know.

'Thought not,' he said grimly. 'Another kindergarten conspiracy.'

'Charlotte mentioned the idea last week,' Lucy explained. 'Pestered me about it, really, as has been her wont just lately. And I told her specifically not to say anything to Ellie until I'd thought about it and decided if—'

'If it was a disastrous idea,' he finished for her. 'Which, evidently, you did.'

'No,' she answered reluctantly. 'I'd love to have Ellie down. I just didn't know...' She hesitated, then plumped for honesty. 'If you'd regard your inclusion in the invitation as a blessing or a curse.'

There was a brief silence at the far end of the phone, then he answered carefully, 'You know, that really depends on how *you* would view it, Lucy.'

That wasn't hard, and she answered simply, although it took courage, 'I'd like you to come. Very much.'

By the time Lucy put down the phone ten minutes later, it had all been arranged—an entire weekend with Malcolm and Ellie at Lucy's parents', when the most she had hoped for had been a single evening. She didn't know whether to start singing or groaning.

On hearing about the plan the following morning, Charlotte was in no such quandary. She literally rubbed her hands together with glee, then proceeded to jump up and down in excitement, and did that at intervals for most of the week. On Thursday night, Lucy extracted from her an eager admission of the wonderful new theory she'd concocted with Ellie.

'We'll all have *such* a good time that we won't want to be separated any more, so you and Ellie's daddy will decide to get married.'

Charlotte didn't bother to tell Malcolm about this idea. Somehow, she suspected that he would already have heard the entire thing from Ellie.

As long as he doesn't think that's what I'm hoping

for as well. An adult just can't get away with being so
blatant about it…

Lucy's parents welcomed their new guests with open
arms on Friday night, just as Charlotte and Lucy had
both known they would. It was nine o'clock by the time
they arrived, as Malcolm hadn't been able to leave work
early.

They'd eaten an evening picnic at the municipal park
in Braidwood on the way through, having passed
through several areas of stark, fire-blackened bush and
ground covered in ghostly blue-grey ash on the way.
More than two weeks after the fires, the air still smelled
strongly of burnt-out wood.

Now the girls were ready for bed. It was a three-
bedroom house, which made for some moments of mild
embarrassment as Charlotte and Ellie didn't understand
at first why they couldn't share.

'Because then Mummy and Ellie's dad would have
to share a room, and that wouldn't work,' Lucy tried to
explain.

'Why not?' Ellie wanted to know.

'Because big people need their privacy,' Granny cut
in very firmly. 'Now, off with you, or you'll be too tired
for the beach in the morning.'

Later, over a cup of tea once the two girls were settled, she told Lucy and Malcolm, 'And I think I'd better
order both of you off to bed as well, or you won't be
fit for the beach either.'

The next day was glorious. Along this part of the
coast, the water temperature was often at its warmest in
March, and the girls were able to play in the surf and
on the sand for the whole morning without getting cold.
Sunburn, in fact, was still the greater danger, and both

parents made sure that their daughters were well covered in the protective long-sleeved bathing suits that most Australian children wore these days, as well as sunhats and sun screen. The adults were similarly covered.

Lying back on her towel on the sand, Lucy would have given a lot to know what Malcolm was thinking as he watched the children's play on his way back from the surf.

We fit together so well, the four of us, she thought. And my parents like him already, and they love Ellie, of course. Who could fail to love Ellie? It seems *obvious*. Yes, it seems as obvious to me as it does to Ellie and Charlotte, but he's seeing a lot more than that. It would be the worst mistake in the world to marry because we *look* like a family. He knows that. And I have to try and see it the way he does.

Not easy. Malcolm was quite close now, lying on his back after his vigorous swim, with droplets of sea water still rolling down his bare sides. His hair was wet and messy and dark, and his chest and shoulders glistened from the fresh layer of sunscreen he'd just applied. He looked strong and fit and at ease in his body.

If they'd been lovers, or husband and wife, she would have rolled towards him to caress those smooth, undulating shapes of muscle and sinew and bone, but with only the tentative accord that existed between them, she couldn't be nearly so bold.

Are his feelings changing at all? she wondered. Will he ever feel the way I do…the way I have for so long? Or did Bronwyn's death kill that in him for ever?

'Hello!' said Lucy's mother brightly at that moment.

She had Lucy's father following closely in her wake, and they were both dressed for swimming, after staying up at the house for an extra hour so that Dad could do some work in the garden.

'Looks so inviting,' said Mum. 'But if you two would like a swim together first,' she offered, 'go ahead. Dad and I will watch the girls.'

'I've just had one, thanks,' Malcolm returned. 'Lucy, it's your turn. Have a go with your mum and dad. That boogie-board is great. I'll help with that "swimming pool" they're working on.'

'So will I,' Dad decided. 'I like to get baking hot before I take the plunge.'

'You'll realise in a minute, Malcolm,' Lucy's mother came in, 'that taking the plunge is not something he does often. This is only the third time since we moved here that I've got him into his swimming costume.'

'I'm working up to it,' Dad protested. 'Maybe I'll just paddle in the girls' pool.'

So Lucy and her mother took their boogie-boards and waded out into the surf, while the two men joined the girls and turned a rather modest hole about half a metre across into a huge gouge in the sand, with mountainous sand walls all around it.

A cynic might have suggested that the men were soon enjoying themselves even more than the children, and Mum laughed out loud a few minutes later as both she and Lucy heard Dad saying enthusiastically, 'Dig it out a bit more on that side, Mal, and, quick, build up the wall. The tide's coming in, I reckon. We're going to lose the lot if we're not careful. Hang on, where's that shovel?'

'Getting on together like there's no tomorrow,' she commented to Lucy.

'What, the girls? Yes, they do. They hardly ever squabble.'

'I meant Alan and Malcolm.'

'Oh. Right.'

There was a silence. They were wading out again
after an exhilarating ride in. Lucy rinsed the sand off
her board so that it wouldn't graze her stomach, then
held the board ready again as they both waited for a
good wave.

Mum said tentatively, 'That's important, isn't it? For
the two of them to get on?'

'I—I don't know yet,' Lucy answered lightly. 'We've
really only just started going out together, Mum.'

'But he's Charlotte's father, isn't he, love?'

Lucy gasped and her heart skipped a beat. 'How did
you…?' She'd never suspected that Mum knew.

'I remembered his name,' she said calmly. 'You told
us at the time who you were working for. Perhaps
you've forgotten. You said quite a lot about both of
them at first, Bronwyn and Malcolm, when we talked
on the phone, and then gradually you started saying less
and less, and then she died and you turned up back
home. A couple of months later you told us about
Charlotte. The timing was right. I always knew it wasn't
Brett. Did your…affair…last for a long time?'

'Oh, Mum, no! *No!*' Lucy answered quickly. 'It
wasn't like that. It wasn't an affair!'

A wave swelled and ebbed and both of them automatically raised their boards and let the strong muscle
of water lift their feet briefly from the sand beneath
them as it passed.

'It was just one night…one time…' she went on, 'and
we both felt so terrible about it that I left the next day.'

'I'm glad,' said her mother quietly. 'I wouldn't have
liked to think that my daughter would sleep with a man
behind the back of his dying wife.'

'Oh, it wasn't like that at all! Really, Malcolm isn't the type who'd—'

'It's all right, love,' Mum soothed. 'I didn't think he was. But I knew *something* must have happened. If nothing else, he and Charlotte are so alike in their mannerisms and the shape of their faces. More alike, I think, than he is to Ellie.'

'It took me a while to see that, but now I do,' Lucy agreed.

'And what about Malcolm? He knows, I assume?'

'He does now. He didn't until a few weeks ago. He wants to tell the girls. But I—I'm not ready.'

'It's hard, at their age,' Mum agreed.

'At any age,' Lucy said. 'How do we tell them that they're sisters? We're working towards it, but it may be a few months yet.'

'And is there anything else you're working towards?'

Lucy watched and waited as another wave passed before she answered. It was a big one. They both had to jump and hold onto their boards to keep their heads above water, and were carried several metres closer to shore. The water was fabulous, clear and glassy and invigorating without being truly cold.

'I don't think he wants to get married again, Mum, if that's what you're asking,' she said finally. 'When a man has lost a wife in the way Malcolm lost Bronwyn, so young, it leaves such scars. And as for myself… I've thought about it. For Charlotte's sake, and for me, too, my own needs,' she admitted. 'I couldn't take the instability of anything less.'

'But you do love him?'

'Yes. A pity, isn't it?'

She didn't want to talk about it any more, and an incoming wave was well timed to end the conversation.

Mum was pretty good anyway. She always knew not to say too much. They took the wave together, pulling the boards beneath their stomachs and careering towards the shore on the foaming white crest, to finish with a rather ungainly scramble to their feet as sandy water poured off their legs.

'I should stand up sooner,' Lucy's mother gasped, wearing a big grin. 'But it's such a lovely feeling, zooming in like that, that I always stay on till the end and get my swimsuit full of sand!'

'Same here.'

They laughed at each other, breathless and salty and getting cold, since they'd stood in the water, having that heart-to-heart, for so long. Then they turned to the others, some metres away along the tideline now as there was a slight current in the water, which had pulled them gradually down the beach as they'd surfed.

The two girls were prancing around in the pool, splashing and shrieking. Dad was sitting on the sandy bank, with his elbows on his knees and his head tipped forward. Malcolm was standing in front of him, bending close. They were probably discussing further ambitious plans for the engineering of the 'swimming pool'.

'Enough?' Lucy's mother suggested, watching the foursome.

'I think so,' Lucy agreed.

'It was glorious! I'll tell your dad that he just *has* to—' She stopped, then clutched her daughter's arm. 'Lucy! Lucy!'

'I know,' she agreed tightly, having seen what Mum had at exactly the same time. 'Something's wrong with Dad.'

They both began racing along the hard sand of the

beach at the water's edge. Lucy got there first, and threw down her board. 'What's wrong?'

The girls had realised that something was wrong now, too.

'Grandad's got a pain,' Charlotte said. 'And he can't breathe properly.'

'Malcolm?'

He was still bending over Dad, with a hand on his shoulder, talking to him quietly. 'Just relax. Relax… Breathe steadily and slowly. Is it easing?'

'Starting to. Yes, it's easing. Thank heavens!'

'I'm going to take your pulse.'

'Go ahead.'

Malcolm sat down beside Dad on the mound of sand. Both men were messy with sand and salt and moisture. Dad's lips looked dry, and he was pale and sweating. Malcolm had the sea breeze whipping hair across his forehead. The tide was definitely coming in. Lucy's own breathing was high and shallow with fear now.

A wave threatened the elaborately dug pool, and Malcolm said, 'Let's move you further up the beach in a minute, Alan, and have you lie on a towel for a few minutes.'

'It's his heart, isn't it?' Mum said. Her voice sounded unnatural, high and quavery.

Malcolm looked up at her. 'Yes, Marion, I think it is.'

'Oh, no!' She twisted her fingers together.

'I have my mobile in the pocket of my shorts.' He was looking for it as he spoke. 'I'll ring for an ambulance and they'll get you to hospital, Alan. You're all right,' he insisted gently, 'but we do need to take this seriously.'

'Alan, you shouldn't have done so much in the garden this morning,' Mum said, fear making her tetchy.

'Wasn't the garden. Was this hole thing!' he answered with effort. 'I wanted to make it…really beaut.'

'You did, Grandad,' Charlotte said tenderly, putting a sandy hand on his bare, bony knee and looking up into his face with her big blue eyes. 'You made it the beautest thing I've ever seen.'

'Did I, darling?' He rested a shaky hand on top of his granddaughter's and chafed it to and fro, and Lucy could see the fear in his eyes.

'You're *all right*, Dad,' she told him urgently. 'Malcolm sees this sort of thing all the time, and so do I. We're not letting you go just yet, believe me! There's so much they can do for heart problems these days, and you'll be fine. The pain is easing, isn't it?'

'Yes, but if I move… I *can't* move.'

They all sat with him on the sand for several minutes more, a knot of anxious people. Even the girls stopped playing and tried half a dozen innocent ways of cheering Grandad up. Lucy dimly registered that Ellie was now calling him 'Grandad' as well. 'Here, Grandad, have this shell, too. Isn't it a lovely colour?'

One or two people just arriving at the beach came over to ask if there was anything they could do, but Malcolm, taking quiet but firm control, shook his head. 'We have the ambulance on its way, and I'm a doctor. Everything's fine, thanks.'

Lucy knew that he couldn't be certain of that. She also knew that to suggest to Dad that things *weren't* fine would be disastrous. It was vital to keep a coronary patient from panicking, because if the heart was further stressed by fear…

At last they heard the familiar wail of the siren. 'Busman's holiday for you two,' Dad joked feebly. 'Glad, though. Helps, having you.'

'Don't try to stand up, Dad,' Lucy begged. 'Malcolm's gone to tell them where to come, and they'll have a stretcher.'

'Feel silly, getting carried off the beach.'

But he made no real protest, and Lucy suspected that the pain began to return the moment he tried the slightest exertion. Mum was still breathing as if she might burst into tears at any moment, and she said under her breath as she saw the paramedics approach, 'Oh, hurry! Hurry!'

They did, and he was loaded into the ambulance within a few minutes. Lucy had packed up the beach things and given the boogie-boards to the girls to carry, and they were soon back at the house and changed out of swimming clothes, ready to see Dad at the hospital.

By the time they arrived, the diagnosis was firmer. Nitrates under Dad's tongue had dealt with some of the pain, but not all of it, and he'd received morphine as well. Questioned by the local doctor in the emergency department of the small country hospital, he admitted he'd been having some pain on exertion before this but had assumed it was indigestion.

'What's going to happen, Malcolm?' Mum asked shakily, when Dad was left alone to rest.

'He'll have to go up to Canberra in a couple of days,' Malcolm explained. 'He'll have a coronary angiogram to have a look at exactly where the problem is, and then he'll probably need an angioplasty. If it's more serious, they'll do a bypass. Those are the most likely possibilities, anyway.'

'Oh, Lucy.' Mum turned to her. 'I'm so glad we made the move from Brewarra when we did. We're so much closer to the hospital here, and they would have sent him all the way to Sydney from Brewarra, wouldn't they? For the tests and the procedure?'

'Probably,' Lucy agreed, squeezing her mother's hands.

'Oh, Lucy, thank goodness you and Malcolm were here!'

'I'm sorry, everyone,' Dad said, when they paid him a visit in hospital that evening. 'I've spoiled your weekend.'

'Don't worry about it, Dad,' Lucy said warmly, then teased, 'Just make sure you don't try to dig all the way to China next time. A few thousand metres into the earth's crust is probably deep enough.'

And in a strange way he hadn't spoiled the weekend. He'd added another dimension to it, a deeper layer of connection…because, as Mum's words earlier that afternoon had suggested, Malcolm had fitted into the whole drama as if he'd truly belonged. He'd been able to calm Mum's fears and present a clear picture to Dad. He'd taken the girls on a rock-pool exploration that afternoon while Lucy and her mother had helped Dad settle in properly at the hospital, and he'd taken over the cooking of the evening barbecue without a particle of fuss.

Mum stayed at the hospital after it was time to take the girls home to bed, telling Lucy, 'I'll get a taxi home. I'm going to stay as long as they'll let me.'

'That's till ten,' said the nurse, who'd come to check Dad's pulse and blood pressure.

'Ten.' Mum nodded firmly. 'All right, so expect me at about a quarter past, but not before.'

Lucy only understood why her mother had been so

definite on the subject once the girls were in bed and already asleep at just after eight o'clock. A day of activity and ocean air had tired them both out so thoroughly that they'd dropped off almost as soon as their heads had hit their pillows.

Which left Lucy and Malcolm with at least two hours in which they were essentially quite alone, just as Mum had known they would be.

'Would you fancy a drink?' Malcolm suggested as soon as they'd emerged from their respective rooms.

'Tea? Oh...'

'I didn't mean tea,' he said bluntly. 'I meant a *drink*. I'm thinking of coffee and one—just one—of those highly alcoholic creamy things that you sip out of a tiny glass. Something that's going to go straight to my head and make me a bit light-headed and very sleepy, and the only reason I'll stay awake at all is because of the coffee, which will be rich and fresh and—'

'Stop it!' she groaned. 'You're making it all sound so good that I'll probably weep if we discover there's none in the house.'

'But there is,' he said triumphantly. 'Your father offered me a drink last night while you were in the shower. I was given a guided tour of the possibilities in his liquor cabinet. And your mother made fresh coffee this morning. The beans are in the freezer and the electric grinder is in the cupboard under the stove. There's even...' he was poking around in the pantry as he spoke '...some sort of...' he found a tin and took off the lid '...very wicked-looking chocolate-slice thingy, with, I'd say...' he inhaled the aroma rising from the tin '...walnuts in it. We'll have some of that, too.'

'You ought to have been an insurance salesman,' she said, accusingly. 'You'd have done extremely well, if your success at selling me your supper plan is any guide. You could have stopped before you got to the chocolate slice.'

'And *you* could have held out a bit longer. I was going to offer to bring it all to you on a tray,' he teased, 'if that was what it took to persuade you.'

She groaned again.

Fifteen minutes later, there they sat with their supper and soft music playing, and both of them so aware of each other that it was no surprise at all when he slid closer to her on the large, soft leather couch and wrapped his arms around her.

'Oh, Lucy, what is it about you?' he whispered, brushing his lips against her hair and her ear and her neck. 'What *is* it? You're like the harbour and I'm the boat, and there's been a huge storm and I'm limping into port with my mast broken, and there you are, tranquil and safe and there for me.'

He turned her face towards his with the caress of his fingers along her jaw, and pressed his forehead against hers. Then he sat back just a little and brushed the hair from her forehead, as if needing to brush away the shadow it made so that he could see her eyes. He searched them.

What was he looking for? she wondered, holding herself very still.

She could almost hear her own heart beating, and could definitely hear his breathing, steady but a little ragged at the edges.

Surely he's not in any doubt that I feel the way he does? I haven't tried to hide it. I haven't tried to hold back. Yet I hope I haven't been too eager either.

She studied him just as intently, taking in the slightly lived-in look of his face. A crease here and there, especially around his sensitive mouth, one or two tiny scars from childhood chickenpox, eyes that showed both pain and laughter in their misty grey depths.

'Are you going to kiss me properly, Malcolm?' she said softly, seeing enough in his face to give her the encouragement she needed.

'Definitely.'

'Good.'

His mouth came down on hers unhurriedly, tasting her like a connoisseur of fine wine, teasing her with the delicacy of its touch, then giving in once more to what they both wanted. After a few minutes there was no room for teasing any more. Their mouths ravaged each other hungrily, tasting the chocolate and the coffee and the brandy and the cream, until they were both swollen and tingling and dizzy and numb. Different sensations in different parts of them, adding up to one magical, sensual whole.

Mouth on mouth was not enough any more. She felt the strength of his arousal against her, and the straining eagerness of her breasts for his touch. His hand forced its way between their two bodies and she eased away from him, happy to give him the space he wanted.

'Buttons,' he murmured huskily, his fingers whispering against her collar-bone. 'I've always liked buttons. They create…' he undid the first one '…a wonderful sense of anticipation…' He undid the second, and the third, and the fourth, until her figure-hugging angora knit cardigan fell open to reveal her lacy silver-grey bra.

He could be in no doubt now that he'd aroused her. The tight nubs of her nipples puckered against the soft cups, and her breathing had unravelled into threads of irregular sound. Shamelessly, he let his gaze linger there and she hid nothing, just waited, forcing back her body's impatience, until he was ready to touch her.

And, oh, he was wicked about it! How could he be so wicked? To use just one finger like that, trailing down from her throat to the exposed and achingly sensitive valley between her breasts. Two fingers now, wandering a little from side to side, making every pore in her skin tighten and her chest heave as she abandoned any attempt to control her breathing.

'Hmm,' he whispered. 'Looks like I'm going to have to find my way around to the back…'

He slid both hands, warm and wantonly exploring, around her body, deliberately brushing against the undersides of her breasts, until he reached the fastening of her bra. It took him a good minute to work out how to unhook it, using touch alone, and he laughed softly at his own clumsiness.

'Still,' he said huskily, 'I always feel it doesn't show a man in a very good light if he's *too* adept at this particular manoeuvre.'

Lucy laughed and nodded, her eyes half-closed like a cat's. 'I would do it for you, but—'

'But every man needs a challenge.'

'And every woman needs— Oh…!'

'This?' he said.

'Yes!'

His hands, *very* adept now, slipped the soft angora from her shoulders and flicked each bra strap down, too, so that within seconds she was bared to his touch. His patience suddenly evaporated, and hers was long gone. All they both wanted was his hands on her breasts, his silken fingers moulding their firm swell and the balls of his thumbs activating those hardened nipples until they throbbed. His mouth, too…

Her control was fast ebbing away, and her hands seemed to have a life of their own. They raked through his hair as he nudged and nuzzled against her breasts with heated lips. They kneaded the muscles of his back and drew shudders from him as she used her nails to lightly scrape the sensitive skin at his sides.

They wandered to the waistband of his jeans and slid around to the fastening at the front, and she began to conclude that a man had no right to complain about undoing a bra. Unzipping a pair of jeans when the owner of those jeans was in the state that Malcolm was in at the moment was—

He convulsed without warning and twisted away from her, doubling over and pushing her hands from his body at the same time.

'I'm sorry,' he gasped. 'This is— I didn't mean at all to let it get this far.'

'I did, and further, too,' she told him openly. 'At least, I hadn't planned it, but…I'm *not* sorry, Malcolm, and you don't need to be.'

He propped his feet on the rustic wooden coffee-table and hugged his arms around his knees.

'I'm not,' he said. His tone was abrupt, but she recognised that he wasn't angry. It was the fact that he was engaged in such a titanic struggle for control. 'I'm not sorry it happened, but— Hell! We're really no good at making boundaries for ourselves in this area, are we, Lucy? I thought I could. I made one in my head. I had it planned when I kissed you— Stupid word! When my mouth drank you in, ravished you— No, there *aren't* words! This was going to be lazy, and easy, and nice, and wasn't going to get anywhere *near* the point where it would have to end in bed. But it did. So quickly!'

'Does it matter?'

There was a long silence. Finally, he turned to her, his eyes narrowed and glittering with emotion.

'Yes. It matters. I won't sleep with you, Lucy, without having anything to promise you at the end of it. I did it to you once before, in the worst possible way. You're such a generous person. I think you still don't realise how culpable I was that night, and *not* because I betrayed Bronwyn, but because I betrayed *you*. I had nothing to offer you. I was only taking. Using you— your energy, your warmth, your generosity, your strength. Hell, like some awful B-grade sci-fi film where parasitic aliens use humans as their hosts.'

'Oh, *Malcolm*.'

'Are you *laughing*?'

'Yes! Aliens? But, no… No, not really.' She was shaking, actually. Or was that him? Both of them, perhaps.

With his feet still propped on the coffee-table and his upper body twisting to face her, he looked awkward, angular. She longed to use her hands again to massage the tension out of him, like kneading a stubborn batch of dough, and as always, *always*, she only wanted to help him, to ease his pain and douse the smouldering fire of his damning self-judgement.

'Go to bed,' he ordered her gently.

'I—'

'*Please*, Lucy. Let me take control here, to do what's right. Trust me, listen to me, and stop *giving*. That's an *order*, all right?'

She nodded, her neck feeling stiff and painful with the movement. 'All right.'

'Good.'

Her capitulation didn't seem to give him any pleasure. He looked grim and determined, as if his inner vision was fixed on some point in the far distance that he was desperate to reach despite incalculable pitfalls on the way. He hardly seemed to notice her preparations for bed, as she cleared away the remnants of their decadent supper, checked on Charlotte, drank a glass of water, switched on the outside light to guide her mother's feet up the front path.

Even when she said goodnight, it drew only a gruff, sketchy echo from him, and she ached, physically, with rejection as she lay in the twin bed next to her daughter's.

Full understanding was settling on her like a winter frost. He won't sleep with me because he knows I want more—the full package, commitment and marriage—and he knows he can't give it. That part of him died with Bronny. He's trying to be kind. I wonder if he's right.

At the moment, burning for him like this, I'd rather take what he *does* have to offer, no matter how little it is, but maybe that would only make it worse in the long run when it came to an end. He said I was too generous. He's wrong. I'm greedy and grasping and I just want to grab as much of him as I can get!

She was still lying awake, with all this churning through her mind over and over again, when her mother let herself quietly into the house at twenty-five past ten.

CHAPTER NINE

LIFE went on, merciless, marvellous process that it was. Dad spent two nights in hospital down at the coast, before being driven by patient transport up to Canberra on Monday morning. Mum followed in the car, and settled into the spare room at Lucy's.

Dad's coronary angiogram, done the next day, showed that the blockage in his arteries was minor. Then an angioplasty, performed by pushing a balloon catheter through the two partially blocked vessels, was successful in treating the problem. Mum looked ten years younger when Dad was discharged. They spent several more days with Lucy, before driving back home.

Charlotte and Ellie were both promoted to 'blue-spot' readers at school, and could count to ten in Japanese. Lucy followed them as far as five—*'Itchy, knee, san, she, go'*— and then gave up. They seemed to have dropped their little strategy of leaving things at each other's houses on purpose, but they certainly hadn't given up plotting and planning altogether.

On more than one occasion, Lucy came to Charlotte's room to call them both for an afternoon snack, only to hear their excited conversation abruptly end the moment she opened the tightly closed door.

'What's this all about?' she asked once, as innocently as she could.

'Our birthdays,' Ellie answered, far too quickly. The child could think on her feet, no doubt about that!

So could Charlotte. 'Yes, we're going to have the most *fabulous* parties,' she said.

But hers wasn't until November, and Ellie's was in January, both many months away. Hmm.

Work had its ups and downs, too. Two patients provided a satisfying feeling of closure which was often lacking in an area like emergency medicine.

First, on a windy morning in mid-May, Mary Sisley turned up in the waiting room with her niece and acted, rather endearingly, as if she owned the place. She must have been a model patient in rehab, as she was managing her new prosthesis beautifully, and a long, voluminous and very pretty skirt ensured that no one would have guessed it wasn't her own leg.

'I told her, Black Mountain Hospital, Accident and Emergency Department,' she explained loudly to Wendy Boyle, who was triaging each patient that day, as she had been on the day when they'd first met Mary. 'Lots of bleeding. Don't muck about. That needs stitches, my girl. Sister Lucy Beckett and Dr Malcolm Lambert. So here we are!'

'I cut it on a can of cat food,' the younger Mary explained to Lucy, once she'd been taken to a cubicle. She showed Lucy the pad of flesh below her thumb, where a nasty-looking gash was rapidly soaking a makeshift wad of bandage.

'It *does* need stitches,' Lucy agreed. 'Dr Lambert will be here in a minute.'

Normally, he wouldn't have handled a routine case like this, and neither would Lucy, but things were relatively quiet and Wendy had murmured to Lucy, 'I thought you'd both like to have a chat to her and see how she is. I'll never forget that day!'

'I did have a nightmare about it a couple of weeks ago,' Lucy admitted.

To Mary Jones, in one of the treatment cubicles, she explained, 'You'll have a local anaesthetic, which will sting a bit, but the stitches themselves shouldn't hurt. It looks like a clean cut, so I doubt whether Dr Lambert will suggest antibiotics. He'll use something topical on the wound itself.'

Mary's aunt patted her arm condescendingly and said, 'See!' It was as if her own visit to A and E had been an unqualified success and little black guns hadn't entered the affair at all.

Malcolm came in. 'Ah!' he said. 'Our friend Mrs Sisley. How are you getting about, Mary?'

'Oh, I move like the breeze.'

'Yes,' retorted her niece with a good-humoured frown. 'You moved like the breeze right into me in the kitchen this morning, and that's how I cut my hand!'

'But I make myself useful...'

'Oh, you do, Auntie Mary, you do,' the younger Mary said soothingly. 'She's split a *huge* pile of kindling for our slow-combustion stove over the past two weeks.'

'I did it sitting down!'

'We're set for the whole winter now.'

The cut hand was soon carefully stitched. There was no muscle or tendon damage, and the two Marys went on their way.

'Strong characters, both of them,' Malcolm commented to Lucy.

'I know. It's not everyone who can live with mental illness the way Mary's niece is.'

'And you can see how hard Mrs Sisley is trying. She appreciates the support. I doubt whether she'll do anything to jeopardise it—like stopping her medication—if she can possibly help it.'

Their second familiar patient, a week later, was also dealing confidently yet realistically with his condition.

'I remembered what you said about Chiari symptoms,' Sam Ackland said. 'And I think this is them. My doctor's on holidays at the moment, and I don't know his locum, so I thought I'd rather come to you. If it *is* Chiari, then I'll probably need to be admitted anyway, won't I?'

'I expect so,' Malcolm agreed, while Lucy stood by in case she was needed. 'What are the symptoms?'

'My legs feel weaker than usual, and tighter, too. My scoliosis has got worse quite quickly, even though I try to do my exercises.'

'Hmm. That doesn't sound like Chiari.'

They were both using the medical shorthand for a brain malformation common in spina bifida patients. Lucy didn't know much about it, only that it meant part of the brain was too low down towards the neck. It was named after the German pathologist who had discovered it over a hundred years earlier. In many cases it could be treated, and it could manifest itself unpredictably. In Sam's age group it was usually the result of a problem with the shunt that drained excess cerebrospinal fluid.

Malcolm asked Sam, 'Any neck pain?'

'No, not really.'

'Difficulty in swallowing?'

'No. Heck, how do you guys keep all this stuff straight?'

'Good question! I'm glad *you* kept it straight enough to be suspicious and come in. It really doesn't sound like Chiari, but it *does* sound like something. Possibly something called… No, I won't get you any more confused with names! But I think you may have developed some fluid-filled cysts in your spinal cord.'

'Doesn't sound good,' Sam joked, but Lucy could see that he was tense now.

He knew enough about shunt failure to know it could be dealt with. This was something new. She reached out and took his hand and, instead of pushing it away—as she'd half expected him to—he clung to it, with his eyes fixed on Malcolm's face. Against her own wrist, she could feel the tickle of his new medical alert bracelet.

'I thought your big lecture a while ago was about how I'd be OK if I took my condition seriously,' he accused, his voice a little shaky.

'And you did take it seriously, and you will be OK,' Malcolm answered firmly. 'It's just another drainage problem, basically. Maybe it's the new shunt and Nick Blethyn will need to tinker with that a bit more. Or maybe the shunt, even if it's performing well, isn't adequate and you'll need a second one lower down to drain fluid from the spinal cord.'

'Shunt stuff.' Sam nodded. 'OK. You're right. I can handle shunt stuff. Roll me on in, then. Surgery, here I come!'

'Hey,' Malcolm said. 'Hang on a tick! Want to hear a bit more about how you're doing first, since you've allowed us the luxury of time for a chat this visit.'

'Full run-down?'

'Full run-down, thanks!'

It turned out that Sam wasn't living on his own any more. He'd moved back to his parents' house.

'Felt like a failure for a while,' he admitted, 'but I've got another plan now. I'm really working on doing everything for myself back at home. Then in two years, when my brother's left school, we're going to share a place. And hopefully I've stopped growing now, so I won't have any more of these rotten brain problems once this new thing is fixed up.'

'That does seem the most likely explanation for why you've had such a series of things over the past couple of years,' Malcolm agreed.

Lucy phoned up to the neurological ward to check the availability of a bed, and Sam was taken up an hour later. He would have some tests done later that day in order to map the way his shunt was functioning and pinpoint the location of fluid build-up in his spine. Lucy probably wouldn't see him again. For his sake, she *hoped* she wouldn't.

It was the same with most of their patients. This department was a way station. You did the best you could for them, then sent them on, either to a ward or to surgery or back home. The ones you *did* see repeatedly were usually not people whom you could welcome warmly. Drug overdoses, delirious alcoholics…

Time and again, Lucy helped Malcolm fight grimly for a patient's life when some might have argued that it wasn't worth the effort.

'There's always a chance something might happen to turn a person around,' he told a new nurse one day.

They were dealing with a heroin overdose, the third time this particular patient had turned up in as many months. Malcolm injected a drug which would act quickly and effectively to block the uptake of the heroin, but unfortunately on this occasion more was needed. The thin young woman had breathed in her own vomit and had contracted aspiration pneumonia. She would need to be admitted to the respiratory ward and put on antibiotics, but whether this enforced break from her drug would help her break the cruel habit remained to be seen.

As she was wheeled away, Malcolm said to Lauren Sandler, 'Don't take on the task of giving up hope on their behalf. That's wrong. And it's not your decision.'

Giving up hope. The words stuck in Lucy's mind. When it came to her feelings about Malcolm it was, as he'd said in a very different context, 'not her decision'.

Because she simply didn't have a choice. To stop loving him might have been the sensible approach, the road to self-preservation, but she just couldn't do it. Her love had been kindled into existence more than six years ago, and it was as much a part of her now as was her love for Charlotte, the daughter they shared.

You couldn't make yourself stop loving someone just because it was painful.

And, of course, it wasn't always. Some of the time—much of the time—it was fabulous. They went out together quite a lot, but the presence of two little daughters rendered each occasion into something safe and innocently fun, with none of the raw, conflicting emotions that had flared down at Lucy's parents' place in March.

Autumn in Canberra was a glorious season, the sort of open secret which all the locals knew and the tourists were happy to discover. Crisp mornings softly slid into bright blue days, with the evergreen eucalypts contrasting against the European and North American trees as they flared into rich autumn colour.

Against this backdrop, Malcolm and Ellie and Lucy and Charlotte went to the adventure playground at Kambah, where they slid down the giant slide and zoomed on the 'flying fox'. They had a sausage sizzle at Weston Park and sandwiches in the botanic gardens, and on an unseasonably warm day in late May they strolled through the outdoor sculpture garden at the National Gallery, looking at bronze figures and abstract metallic shapes, and the two girls got happily saturated in the Japanese fog sculpture.

Lucy and Malcolm stood in the cool, ever-changing drifts of its mist for a minute or two as well, and laughed as hard as Ellie and Charlotte, although they drew the line at shrieking and running.

On a handful of occasions, these daylight pleasures spilled over into the evening, when Jenny or her daughter would babysit, either at Lucy's or at Malcolm's, and the two adults would go out to dinner or live music or a movie. Each time, it was easy enough to use Jenny or Clare as a buffer between them at the end of the evening, with diligent parental questions about bedtime and behaviour.

It could have happened the other way, too. It would have been very easy to usher the babysitter out the door, close it firmly and have an hour…two hours…or the whole night…alone together as they willingly explored the vibrant landscape of their physical connection.

But it didn't happen. Lucy could read Malcolm very easily on the issue. The chemistry between them was stronger than ever, but he wasn't going to act on it no matter what it cost him to maintain that control. As for what it cost her…

In this way, they reached the end of May. Daylight saving had ended. The first frost had come and gone. The nights were drawing in much earlier now. Winter was on the doorstep.

Lucy was thinking this as she moved around her kitchen one Friday night, cooking a spaghetti sauce and pasta and tossing a salad for the evening meal. It was only just after half past five, but already, looking out of the window above the kitchen sink, it was almost dark.

Charlotte was still in the back garden, and she probably wasn't quite warmly enough dressed now. She had been very busy and very self-contained after school today.

'No snack,' she'd said. 'We made pancakes at Afters.'

'Change out of your uniform, please.'

'I have, already. Can I go outside?'

'Back yard?'

'Yes.'

'Then of course.' Since the back garden was completely fenced, Lucy had no qualms about letting her play there alone.

It gave her a very peaceful half-hour until the time had come to start the spaghetti. She began to tackle the difficult pattern on the front of the pullover she was knitting for Charlotte, and kept a background awareness of her daughter's movements. Quite a bit of toing and froing.

The back screen door banged numerous times, and once Lucy asked, 'What is it you're playing so busily?'

'Dolls. They've discovered an island, but there are pirates.'

Which sounded fine. But it was time to come inside now. She called this information from the back door, and a voice in the bushes answered, 'Not yet.'

'Yes. Yet. I bet you don't have a jacket on.'

'I'm not cold.'

Lucy sighed. 'Two more minutes, just so you can finish up the game.'

'OK.' And obediently, after a somewhat stretchy two minutes, here she was.

And here was someone else, too, at the front door, not bothering with the bell but hammering so loudly and urgently that Lucy had a moment of sheer panic and a vivid flashback to that day over two months ago when Mary Sisley had attacked her with the gun. There was definitely a limit to what post-traumatic counselling could achieve! The hammering continued, and she didn't dare to answer.

Then she heard Malcolm's voice. 'Lucy! Lucy!'

He lunged inside the moment she opened the door, and he was white and shaking and completely distraught. Only one thing could have made a parent look like that. Lucy's legs seemed to turn to rubber and her throat was so tight she could barely breathe. It was as if all the oxygen had suddenly been taken out of the air.

'It's Ellie, isn't it?' she managed. 'What's happened?'

'She's gone. Just *gone*, Lucy! I've called the police. They're going door to door and searching up in the nature reserve as well, through all the part that was burnt and the thicker bush as well. Jenny is utterly devastated. I gave her a sedative.'

'You mean it happened while—?'

'It must have,' he confirmed, striding through into her living area with a restless purpose that had nothing to fix itself to. He wheeled around, and she saw the agony in his face as she'd seen it six years ago, more than once. 'I got home a bit early and asked where she was. Playing in her room, Jenny said. Jenny was in the kitchen. It wasn't her fault. She was cooking curry. I *hate* her for cooking curry while my child went missing!'

He swore painfully.

'We've tried to think,' he went on. 'To work it out.

She *can't* have been abducted from her room. She must have gone outside. You know how they're always messing around with sticks and leaves, or they leave their toys out there. And Jenny didn't hear her go. And for some reason she didn't come back, but whether it's that she's got lost in the darkness, or…or…'

'And you've looked,' Lucy said stupidly, 'and called?'

'Of *course*!' he rasped. 'All through the house. I thought perhaps she was playing hide and seek and fell asleep in a cupboard. And we've looked in the garden. Under the house. Up the back, although she's been told never to go through the back gate and anyhow it's kept locked. To both the next-door neighbours, even though she only knows them slightly and they don't have kids and I doubt she'd ever go there. We searched and called for a good twenty minutes or more before we realised it was real. I kept thinking that in another minute I'd be clutching her and scolding her at the same time for giving us a silly scare, but she really was gone.

'Now that twenty minutes is torturing me. If it turns out to make a difference… And who knows how long she'd been gone before I got home? I hate Jenny. No, I don't. Of course I don't. Lucy, this is my worst nightmare in living form, and I'm going mad. Anyone could have taken her by this time. I came here to ask—'

'To ask Charlotte.' Lucy nodded quickly, as if finishing his sentences for him might spare him a fraction of the pain.

Back to this again. Sparing Malcolm from pain. Only this time hers was almost as acute. She'd loved Ellie as a fragile newborn, and now she'd come to love her as a six-year-old child. And Ellie was Charlotte's half-sister.

'She might have an idea,' Malcolm was saying. 'Something they've talked about. Running away to join the circus, or something.'

'I know. They're always—'

'I love their vivid imaginations—'

'But not today,' she agreed. 'Today I wish they were the most—'

'Ordinary, unadventurous girls in the world.' His voice shook.

'Charlotte? Charlotte, love…'

No answer. For one horrible moment, Lucy looked down a gun-barrel of stark fear. She and Malcolm both heard the keening of an ambulance siren on its way to the hospital, and she shuddered. But then the sliding door to Charlotte's room rumbled slowly open and there she was, staring up with huge eyes.

'Ellie's daddy came,' Charlotte said, stating the obvious.

'Yes, darling,' Lucy answered, 'because we need to know. Have you and Ellie talked about anything lately, like…like climbing Black Mountain in the dark, or running away to join the circus?'

'No…'

'No?'

'No.' She shook her head vigorously. Dark golden blonde hair went flying back and forth. Then big eyes looked steadily upwards again.

'Because, you see…' How much to tell her? How to tell it? 'Ellie isn't at home, and Ellie's dad is worried.'

'Not very worried.'

'Yes, *very* worried.'

'But she'll be all right.'

'Can I talk to her?' Malcolm was coming up behind

them. Lucy could hear his shaky breathing even from several metres' distance.

'I've already asked,' she said, turning to him. She wanted to hold him, but he looked so tight, as if he were encased in bands of steel. She knew he couldn't have borne any touch at that moment. He'd have pushed her away.

'I know.' He nodded jerkily. 'But I have to ask her myself.'

There was a ring at the door, deflecting their attention. Hurrying to answer it, Lucy found that her mind was jangling with conflicting hope and fear. No news was good news. Who would this be?

The police. 'Is this—?'

'Yes, Malcolm is here.' She practically pulled the two uniformed officers inside. 'Does this mean—?'

'I'm afraid not.' The older of the two men shook his head. 'But—'

Malcolm came up behind him. She felt his hand clutch at her bare forearm, where she still had her sleeves rolled up from washing the cooking dishes. His fingers were clammy and ice-cold.

'We have had one report from someone in Carinya Street, just round the corner from you, Dr Lambert,' the older officer said. 'A child fitting Ellie's description running along the footpath at about five o'clock. Perhaps a bit later.'

Malcolm looked at his watch. 'Now it's six. No one else saw anything?'

'We're still checking. But feel the frost in the air. People are inside by that hour, not hanging around outside. They've just got home from work, or they're not home yet. They're cooking. It's getting dark. The fact that no one saw anything—'

'I know.' Malcolm nodded. 'Doesn't mean—'

'*Anything*, really,' Lucy came in shakily. Malcolm's fingers still made a chilly bracelet on her arm. She wanted to lean against him, *hold* him. The need in her was even stronger now.

'Don't be worried, Ellie's daddy, *please*,' begged a little voice.

Four adults turned in her direction, and there was a sudden silence and the faintest dawning of hopeful possibility. The younger of the two police officers, who looked of an age to have a kindergarten child himself, squatted down.

'But aren't you worried, Charlotte?'

'Yes,' she replied promptly.

'Then why don't you think we should be?'

'I don't want Ellie's dad to be upset.'

'But if she's missing…' He paused deliberately, and the adult gazes now fixed on Charlotte were expectant and searching and just slightly accusatory.

She gazed back for a long moment…then wavered…and crumbled…and cried. 'She's not missing,' she sobbed. 'She's in the shed. She's going to live there.'

'The shed?' Malcolm barked hoarsely. 'We don't have a— You mean *here*?'

'Yes. Here. In our shed.'

'That's almost three kilometres she must have run,' Lucy murmured.

'We've made it all lovely, with pillows and blankets and—'

No one waited to hear any more. Malcolm had already flung himself out of the back door, stumbling down the steps on long legs that would scarcely hold him.

'Ellie!' he was yelling. 'Ellie, answer me, are you there?'

Hard on his heels, Lucy and the two policemen heard, 'Yes, and I'm *cold*, and I'm wheezy, and I forgot my inhaler, and this shed isn't nice in the dark after all.'

In the background, the older policeman pulled out his walkie-talkie and unleashed a short burst of economical police jargon. Relief was conveyed in the tone rather than the words or the body language.

Malcolm was less reticent about showing what he felt. 'Ellie, you must never, *ever* leave home without telling me, ever, *ever* again!'

Lucy heard the sob in his throat and watched his knees buckle as he squatted down. Ellie had come stumbling out of the shed and into his arms with her torch beam quavering. It was quite dim. The little thing must have had it on continuously since she'd arrived, and its batteries were giving out already. Lucy recognised the torch. It normally lived under her own kitchen sink. She wondered grimly how long it had been gone.

Malcolm had pulled Ellie's inhaler from his pocket. He must have grabbed it in a hurry at home with some dim—and, as it turned out, accurate—notion that it might be needed. He didn't have the spacer, but Ellie was managing well without it, drawing in a deep breath as he instructed her, and then another. 'OK, darling girl, OK, that's good. You'll stop wheezing soon. That cold, damp air in the shed isn't any good for you at all, is it?'

Peering into the shed, Lucy saw that with sunny daylight coming in through its single window, it might indeed have looked 'all lovely', as Charlotte had said. Had she achieved all this today? Or had the plan been in train for days?

No, it was weeks, she concluded, thinking back on those excited sessions with the door shut in Charlotte's room and the busy activity in the garden.

'My fault,' she said under her breath. 'I've been meaning to clear this out for weeks, and instead I haven't even looked in here. It still has all our boxes from the move. Well, Charlotte and Ellie have done half the work for me!'

The cement floor was freshly swept. Boxes and tools were piled neatly around the walls. In the centre, there were several pillows and cushions on the floor, as well as a picnic rug and a sleeping bag, and all the toy dishes and cutlery. Provisions, too. Water in an old milk container. Sandwiches. Cereal. A flask of milk. A juice box.

A six-year-old's idea of all the necessities of survival, in other words, but the lonely reality of the place after dark on a cold autumn evening had Charlotte marvelling at Ellie's bravery in sticking it out even as long as she had, torch notwithstanding.

Malcolm had his face buried in Ellie's spun gold hair, and he was still shaking. Lucy reached out and ran her hand across his shoulders, then left it there, kneading the strong, solid flesh gently. When he straightened at last, and her hand fell away, she didn't even know if he'd felt her touch at all.

'Let's all go inside,' he said.

There was a confusing flurry of activity and talk. Malcolm thanked the police for their prompt and sensitive response. They seemed as glad at the harmless, happy ending as if they'd been personally involved. Malcolm rang Jenny and Clare, who were still back at his place, and told them the news.

Lucy put on a saucepan of milk to make hot chocolate for Ellie, drained her pot of spaghetti, looked at its immediate disintegration into total mush and decided to start all over again. She'd need twice as much if Ellie and Malcolm were going to stay for dinner, anyway. And of course they were! Was the ill-fated curry safely switched off at Malcolm's place? she wondered.

Finally, when things were quiet she felt a small hand creep into hers.

Charlotte.

'Are you very, *very* cross, Mummy?'

Where has she been during all this fuss? Lucy asked herself. Hiding in her wardrobe, it turned out, in fear of terrible consequences.

Lucy bent down, aware that Malcolm and Ellie were listening. Malcolm was standing in the kitchen doorway, with Ellie still wrapped safely in his arms as if he didn't plan on letting her go for a long time. Ellie was sipping her hot chocolate.

'I'm not cross, my love,' she said carefully, 'but that's mainly because I'm too relieved and happy to discover that Ellie is safe to feel cross about *anything*. Big people get *terribly* worried when they think their children have gone missing, darling. You're both so precious to us. You must never try and make a great big plan like that without telling us. *Why* did you try and make a place for Ellie to live in the back shed without telling us?'

'Because you would have said no, and we want to live in the same place. We want to be sisters…'

'Oh, my Lord,' Lucy whispered as she heard Malcolm's heartfelt groan, and then the truth just came spilling out, without a moment's pause for thought. 'Darling, you *are* sisters. You're sisters already.'

CHAPTER TEN

'WHY the hell did you say it?' Malcolm demanded two hours later.

The spaghetti had disappeared into four hungry stomachs, the dishes had been washed and put away, stories had been read, teeth had been cleaned, and the girls were both asleep in Charlotte's room. Ellie was wearing one of her own nighties, retrieved from her small stash of running-away clothes in the shed. Somehow, it hadn't occurred to any of them that Ellie and Malcolm should go home.

Now, Malcolm's question burst forth, as if from a pressure cooker, as they stood awkwardly together in the living room. Both adults had been simmering all evening with unsaid things, and an amoeba could have sensed that Malcolm was angry.

Lucy, being a considerably more advanced life form than an amoeba, was acutely sensitive to his anger, and had been waiting for his outburst with both determination and dread.

The two girls had displayed a uniquely six-year-old response to Lucy's earth-shattering revelation. Ellie was thrilled down to her toes about the fact that she now had grandparents, even though, technically, she didn't. And she was quite convinced that she should now start calling Lucy 'Mummy'. Charlotte was already planning to tell everyone at school the moment she saw them.

Thank goodness it was the weekend! Lucy thought.

There might just be time to bring them both back to reality by the end of it.

In summary, disdaining any curiosity whatsoever as to the mechanics of how such a thing could be, they had both simply taken the news as a blindingly obvious piece of serendipity which they had known in their hearts all along.

As perhaps it was.

Malcolm, at the moment, didn't seem to think so, however. He wasn't waiting for Lucy to answer his question. It had apparently been rhetorical in nature, and an answer hadn't actually been required.

Instead, he ploughed on heatedly, 'It's the absolute antithesis of what you said when we talked about it before…and what I knew you still felt every time we've verged on the subject since. You wanted to wait. You *insisted* we wait. And then, all of a sudden, without the slightest prior consultation, you simply come bursting out with it and—' He broke off and his words degenerated into incoherent splutterings.

Lucy faced him without flinching. I didn't *plan* it, Malcolm! Good heavens, ten minutes before that we were both totally distraught. And once we'd found her, and she was safe and sound in that warm kitchen of mine, and I was about to put some hot food into her, I was so light-headed with relief it just came out. And they took it well, didn't they?'

'Aagh! Don't *say* that! *I* always thought that they would take it well. *You* are the one who argued that they wouldn't.'

'No! I never argued that!' she exclaimed, knowing there were some small eddies of illogicality swirling around in her argument but feeling too heated to care about what they were. 'It wasn't their initial reaction I feared, Malcolm. It was what would happen later, when the novelty wore off. I—I'm still afraid about that.'

She frowned, the passionate aftermath of relief and dizzy confidence ebbing swiftly now to allow all her doubts to come flooding back again. What had really changed in their situation? The girls had gone to bed full of wonderful plans about being sisters, but when it came down to cold, hard reality they were still two separate families, with Malcolm's inability to take the risk of full commitment standing in the way of this fact ever changing.

'Terrified, actually,' she added in a small voice.

'Oh, *hell*, Lucy!'

He pulled her roughly into his arms, holding her tightly as he gazed down into her eyes. His kiss was there in his face, so she couldn't have claimed surprise as an excuse. She was angry and emotional and terribly afraid about what she felt, and it would have been far better to stiffen, push away, fight him, *reject* him, but she just couldn't.

His mouth coming down on hers and staying there was just so *right* that she couldn't act on principle or in self-preservation. She returned his kiss, loving everything about it—his taste, the soft strength of his mouth, the words he murmured that she couldn't understand, the way he used his hands to explore and claim her.

Those hands were everywhere, softly grazing the most sensitive parts of her skin as he slid them inside her light cotton pullover, running them over the curves of her hips and breasts, cupping and squeezing her rear end as he pulled her even closer. Oh, yes, he was *claiming* her all right!

All at once, she *did* have the strength to fight, and used her flattened palms to push him away. Her movements were as rough as his had been when he'd taken hold of her.

'I can't do this, Malcolm,' she told him abruptly. 'Not any more. It hurts too much. Tell me what you want from me. Don't leave me guessing. I can't stand it. I feel I know *nothing* about what's happening here, other than the fact that what I feel *hurts*.'

'Oh, Lucy, I'm so sorry,' he whispered. 'This is all my fault, isn't it?'

'Yes,' she agreed helplessly, hugging her arms around herself. Without him, the air seemed cold on her body. 'Totally.'

It was much quieter in the kitchen now. The fridge hummed, and the heating vent in the corner made a little ticking sound every now and again as the gas furnace came on and began to heat the house.

'And you've started wondering if it's remotely worth you sticking this out, haven't you?' Malcolm asked softly.

'Something like that,' she agreed again. 'Except that it doesn't seem as if I have much choice. I—I feel sometimes as if I'd stop loving you if I could, only there's no way in the world that I can. So I'm just *stuck* with it, and—'

'Don't stop loving me, Lucy, *please*,' he said. 'I want you to go on loving me for the rest of your life.'

'But—'

'I want you to marry me.'

'To—'

'*Marry me.*'

'Just like that?' she almost shrieked.

He stilled. 'Damn, is that really how it seems to you? *Just like that?*'

She could only nod tremulously.

'Oh, Lucy…!' He buried his face in her hair and she could feel the passion in every tightened muscle and every throbbing pulse. 'Have you not understood that this is where I wanted it to lead all along?'

'No, I've thought you *couldn't*,' she answered him. 'I've thought that you were telling me you couldn't, ever again, take the risk of something like that, because of Bronwyn.'

'No, Lucy…'

'I thought you wanted to tell the girls that they were sisters but keep the rest of our lives separate, and I hated that thought. It seemed…so hard on them, and *impossible* for me.'

'No, oh, *no*…' He shook his head, then brushed his nose across hers, teasing her by the close contact as he denied her the touch of his lips. 'Nothing like that.'

'No?'

'Please, will you let me tell you about it properly?'

'Oh, please, yes!'

'You see, I understand a lot more about my marriage to Bronwyn than I did six years ago.'

'You've talked to me about it.'

'I had to… But obviously I haven't said enough. It was something that seemed right for us then…perhaps *was* right for us…but it wouldn't have been right now. I don't doubt that we'd have gone on working at it had she lived. Neither of us are…or were…people to give up on something we'd made a commitment to. But with you, I knew I didn't want it to be that way. I didn't want it to be something that we had to grit our teeth and work and work at.'

'All marriages need to be worked at, don't they?'

'But some are more fun to work at than others.' A little smile began to dawn on his face. 'And I wanted to know that what I felt for you, the love I felt—the love I *feel*, huge and real and strong and wonderful—was the right kind of love, the kind that would enrich us for our whole lives, not the kind that would give us a few good years and then fade or twist somehow. And, of course, I *did* know, in my heart, quite soon, but I owed it to four people—you and Charlotte and Ellie and myself—to be utterly and completely certain. That's a pretty heavy responsibility, Lucy, and if Ellie hadn't gone missing today—'

'You mean you were going to make me wait even longer?' she demanded, daring to tease him a little now. She'd wanted this for so long. She'd always known it would be complicated, if it ever came. She hadn't known quite how wonderful it would feel.

'Not much longer,' he admitted. 'My resolve was weakening daily. And, Lucy, you haven't answered me. *Will* you?'

'Oh, Malcolm, I should probably keep you in suspense a little, shouldn't I?' she said helplessly. 'But you know what I'm going to say. I'll marry you. I love you. And it's the only possible way that we can make everything right.'

'We're going to have two very excited little girls,' he said. 'In fact, it's not clear to me how we're going to get them to sleep under different roofs until the wedding.'

'And it's not clear to *me*,' she whispered boldly, pillowing her head on his chest, 'how we're going to get ourselves to sleep under different roofs until the wedding.'

He laughed, an open, happy sound that she loved and that she hoped to hear countless times during their life together. 'In that case, there's really only one question

I have left to ask you, Lucy, my darling. Your place, or mine?'

It was a question that needed more serious consideration in the weeks that followed. There really wasn't any sense in keeping two houses, but Malcolm wouldn't let Lucy sell hers yet.

'Keep it?' he suggested, as they discussed practical plans the day before their wintry July wedding. 'Rent it out?'

'For how long?'

'Oh, about twelve years or so, until Charlotte and Ellie want to declare their independence by moving into it when they finish school.'

'Thinking ahead?'

'I love thinking ahead, when it means thinking about having you in my life,' he murmured.

'What else are you thinking, then?'

They were at his place, and the two girls were in bed. Charlotte and Ellie were both still agonising over the issue of whether to share or to have separate rooms. The house was big enough for either to be an option. Tonight they'd elected to share, and Charlotte was on a mattress on the floor, right next to Ellie.

'Well,' Malcolm said, 'I'm wondering about your wedding dress, and your wedding underwear.'

'Malcolm!'

'Hoping it's not too hard to slip off. Rather looking forward to the process.'

'And?' She could tell there was more.

'Thinking about what we said the other day about more children.'

'We weren't sure, I seem to recall.'

'*I* wasn't, you mean. You were completely sure, only you wouldn't say so.'

'I—'

'Lucy, it's lucky I've learned to read you, because otherwise it might be disastrous that you keep your needs to yourself, the way you do, just in case I don't share them.'

'Oh, Malcolm...'

'You're going to have to stop doing that, you know! And you can start practising now, about the question of children. Be honest.'

'You're right,' she admitted.

'How many?'

'I don't know. Probably two. A boy would be nice. But if you don't want—'

'I *do* want! As soon as I thought about it properly, I knew that I did. Another child together, as imaginative as Ellie and as spirited as Charlotte. And this time a child who doesn't have the darkness that hung over Ellie's birth, and one that you don't have to raise alone. A boy would be fabulous. And doted on utterly by his sisters, I expect.'

'Definitely! Oh, Malcolm, those girls are going to look so lovely in their bridesmaids' dresses,' Lucy answered. 'We're probably crazy to get married in the coldest month of the year, but I couldn't wait, and... OK, if you want me to be honest.' She took a deep breath, ready to get some practice in the honesty that every good marriage required. 'I don't think I can wait about anything, any more, when it comes to you. Can we start working on that new baby very soon?'

'Tonight, perhaps?' he suggested eagerly. 'I mean, we ought to put quite a bit of effort into it, I think. What if we're not very good at making boys?'

She laughed, and kissed him.

'Tonight would be lovely,' she said.

MILLS & BOON®

Makes any time special™

Mills & Boon publish 29 new titles every month. Select from…

Modern Romance™   Tender Romance™

Sensual Romance™

Medical Romance™   Historical Romance™

MAT2

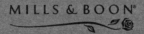

Medical Romance™

GIVE ME FOREVER *by Caroline Anderson*

Mac's return home takes an unexpected turn when he discovers that nurse Ruth Walker has returned at the same time. Once teenage friends, it seems their feelings have changed with a passion…

LISA'S CHRISTMAS ASSIGNMENT *by Jessica Matthews*

Lisa had kept her distance from Dr Simon Travers until asked by colleagues to find him a Christmas gift. Now she was forced to get to know him better…

A REAL FAMILY CHRISTMAS *by Jennifer Taylor*

Nurse Emma Graham had been brought up in a children's home and had never had a real family Christmas—so when Dr Daniel Hutton asked her to join him and his orphaned niece for the day, she readily agreed.

On sale 1 December 2000

MILLS & BOON®

Medical Romance™

BAUBLES, BELLS AND BOOTEES by *Meredith Webber*

Love had grown for Fran when she agreed to marry family friend Dr Henry Griffiths. Knowing how much he wants children, she is distraught at her inability to conceive and decides to find him a new Mrs Griffiths for Christmas.

A KIND OF MAGIC by *Laura MacDonald*

Staff nurse Sophie Quentin's immediate attraction to Benedict, the new registrar, caused her some concern. Even if nothing developed between them, how could she continue her engagement to Miles?

WRAPPED IN TINSEL by *Margaret O'Neill*

Callum Mackintosh's sudden re-appearance after ten years was hardly the Christmas surprise Nan Winters had wanted. But she wasn't in a position to turn down a locum doctor...

On sale 1 December 2000

Available at most branches of WH Smith, Tesco, Martins, Borders, Easons, Volume One/James Thin and most good paperback bookshops 0011/03b

The perfect gift this Christmas from

MILLS & BOON®

3 new romance novels & a luxury bath collection

for just £6.99

Featuring

Modern Romance™

The Mistress Contract
by Helen Brooks

Tender Romance™

The Stand-In Bride
by Lucy Gordon

Historical Romance™

The Unexpected Bride
by Elizabeth Rolls

0011/94/MB7

FREE!

4 Books
and a surprise gift!

We would like to take this opportunity to thank you for reading this Mills & Boon® book by offering you the chance to take FOUR more specially selected titles from the Medical Romance™ series absolutely FREE! We're also making this offer to introduce you to the benefits of the Reader Service™—

       ★ FREE home delivery
       ★ FREE gifts and competitions
       ★ FREE monthly Newsletter
       ★ Books available before they're in the shops
       ★ Exclusive Reader Service discounts

Accepting these FREE books and gift places you under no obligation to buy; you may cancel at any time, even after receiving your free shipment. Simply complete your details below and return the entire page to the address below. ***You don't even need a stamp!***

YES! Please send me 4 free Medical Romance books and a surprise gift. I understand that unless you hear from me, I will receive 6 superb new titles every month for just £2.40 each, postage and packing free. I am under no obligation to purchase any books and may cancel my subscription at any time. The free books and gift will be mine to keep in any case.

MOZEB

Ms/Mrs/Miss/Mr ....Initials...
BLOCK CAPITALS PLEASE

Surname ....

Address...

....

....Postcode ....

Send this whole page to:
UK: The Reader Service, FREEPOST CN81, Croydon, CR9 3WZ
EIRE: The Reader Service, PO Box 4546, Kilcock, County Kildare (stamp required)

Offer not valid to current Reader Service subscribers to this series. We reserve the right to refuse an application and applicants must be aged 18 years or over. Only one application per household. Terms and prices subject to change without notice. Offer expires 31st May 2001. As a result of this application, you may receive further offers from Harlequin Mills & Boon Limited and other carefully selected companies. If you would prefer not to share in this opportunity please write to The Data Manager at the address above.

Mills & Boon® is a registered trademark owned by Harlequin Mills & Boon Limited.
Medical Romance™ is being used as a trademark.